"Explain," Maude whispered, already predicting what he was about to say and dreading confirmation of her suspicions. "What…what was in the paper, Mateo?"

"I debated bringing it but in the end, I thought better of it."

"Why?"

"Because we're engaged."

Maude's mouth fell open and she stared at him in utter shock.

"Sorry?"

"It would seem that I found the love of my life with you and we're engaged."

"No. No, no, no, no…no…"

Cathy Williams can remember reading Harlequin books as a teenager, and now that she is writing them, she remains an avid fan. For her, there is nothing like creating romantic stories and engaging plots, and each and every book is a new adventure. Cathy lives in London, and her three daughters—Charlotte, Olivia and Emma—have always been, and continue to be, the greatest inspirations in her life.

Books by Cathy Williams

Harlequin Presents

Desert King's Surprise Love-Child
Consequences of Their Wedding Charade
Hired by the Forbidden Italian
Bound by a Nine-Month Confession
A Week with the Forbidden Greek
The Housekeeper's Invitation to Italy

Secrets of the Stowe Family

Forbidden Hawaiian Nights
Promoted to the Italian's Fiancée
Claiming His Cinderella Secretary

Visit the Author Profile page
at Harlequin.com for more titles.

Cathy Williams

THE ITALIAN'S INNOCENT CINDERELLA

PRESENTS™

Recycling programs
for this product may
not exist in your area.

ISBN-13: 978-1-335-73928-5

The Italian's Innocent Cinderella

For questions and comments about the quality of this book,
please contact us at CustomerService@Harlequin.com.

Harlequin Enterprises ULC
22 Adelaide St. West, 41st Floor
Toronto, Ontario M5H 4E3, Canada
www.Harlequin.com

Printed in U.S.A.

THE ITALIAN'S INNOCENT CINDERELLA

CHAPTER ONE

'Not what I was expecting…'

Mateo's dark, lazy voice from behind feathered along Maude's spine and she turned around slowly to look at him.

Ever since this arrangement had been made the evening before, Maude had had time to ponder and had come to the conclusion that it was just a terrible idea.

What had possessed her?

Mateo Moreno was her boss. Her billionaire boss. She had spent the past two years climbing the career ladder, doing her utmost, as one of five structural engineers at his prestigious London firm, to impress him with her initiative and drive.

She was thirty-two years old with an exemplary record when it came to productivity and already in charge of a small team. She had always made sure to keep her professional life separate from her private one so why on earth had she been crazy enough to succumb to this reckless adventure? If it could even be called 'adventure', as opposed to 'hare-brained scheme that defied all logic and would end in tears'.

She knew why. Of course she did.

He had caught her in a weak moment. There they'd been the evening before, long after everyone else had left the towering glass building that housed his lavish offices, discussing the latest project and inspecting the scale replica village on the concrete table in his office, when her phone had pinged and she'd read the text that had sent her into a tailspin.

Angus, the plus-one she had roped into her brother's pre-wedding party the following evening, had bailed on her at the last minute. Maude was mystified as to why her brother had to have a pre-wedding party when the actual wedding was only a matter of weeks away, but it had been unavoidable and, that being the case, she had asked Angus to help her out. Matter sorted... until she'd got that text.

His boyfriend had fallen off a ladder. He had decided on a whim to paint the ceiling in their bedroom and had fallen, splintering two bones in his ankle. Why on earth Ron had wanted to paint the ceiling in the first place was a mystery, because he loathed anything to do with DIY. Naturally, there was no way Angus could possibly go to the party while Ron was laid up in hospital, being patched up.

And, in response to a couple of sympathetic questions from Mateo, Maude had done what she had vowed never to do—she had opened up to her boss. He had noted the dismayed expression on her face and had perched on the edge of his desk, tilted his head to one side, pinned those devastating dark eyes on her and had asked what the problem was. And she had opened up.

It was a first. Conversations between them had always revolved around work. Mateo owned multiple companies around the globe. He might be based in London, but he travelled extensively, so their contact was limited to when he was around.

Once a month, he would have a group meeting, and every so often he would summon her to find out the ins and outs of particular projects she had been put in charge of. He seemed to know every detail of every project in her remit, regardless of whether he was physically in the office checking on her work or not. She knew that he was pleased with her progress, because her pay had increased five times in two years, and she now had her own fabulous office with sprawling views across to the Tower of London and the hectic streets below.

Maude had always respected the boundary lines. She had *enjoyed* those boundary lines. Her sights were fixed on her career, and fraternising with the boss had been a big no-no.

But Angus's text...

The prospect of facing eighty-five people...the general chaos...the expensive caterers vying with the expensive florists to see whose creations would be the most admired...not to mention her mother, her gran and various aunts clucking at her unmarried status and asking when she was going to meet some *nice young man*...

A migraine threatened just thinking about it.

Angus as the plus-one by her side would have made the whole extravagant do a little more bearable.

No Angus and the weekend of fun-filled festivities had suddenly loomed like an impending storm.

Thank goodness she had held back from a full scale, hand-wringing confession about her own insecurities, about the way she would be confronted with her life choices and put on the spot by her mother—who always managed to make her feel horrendously self-conscious and a bit of a loser, successful career or no successful career... But she had still confided enough for her to be here now, in a tangle of her own making.

Of course, as Mateo had thoughtfully told her, for him a plus-one situation would come with certain advantages, so the tangle was not *entirely* down to her, but still...

They were here. A party was in full swing. And it was a bad idea.

She plastered a bright, breezy smile on her face and stepped towards him.

Her heart sped up. The broad patio, spacious enough to house several sitting areas, was beautifully lit with fairy lights and lanterns and, in the semi darkness, Mateo was all shadows and angles. Most of the time, Maude could side-line his extraordinary looks. But here, close enough to breathe him in, and without a comforting desk and computer in the background reminding her of those all-important boundaries, her eyes widened and her mouth went dry. He was just so drop-dead gorgeous.

It was a hot, still summer evening and he was wearing a pair of hand-made cream linen trousers, a white shirt cuffed to the elbows and tan brogues. The whole ensemble shrieked the sort of vast wealth that most people could only dream about, including her own comfortably off, middle-class parents. The man was built to turn heads.

He was six-foot-three of dark, brooding, uncompromising Italian beauty, with pitch-dark hair that curled a little too long at the collar and dark eyes that always managed to be expressive without revealing anything at all.

She was suddenly conscious that she was no longer in her usual work uniform. She was wearing a *dress*, something floaty and blue which her mother had bought for her and had then guilt-tripped her into wearing, much to Maude's grudging amusement.

She would have to make sure that this interaction was kept as crisp and formal as possible, given the circumstances. They might not be in an office but it would be a mistake to think he had stopped being her boss. Why compound one mistake by foolishly adding to the tally?

'What were you expecting?' She turned and felt him move to stand next to her as they both surveyed the lavish spectacle in front of them.

'Not this.'

'You mean nothing so lavish?'

'I guess that's one way of putting it.'

'Because I got a first in Engineering at Cambridge, you somehow expected me to come from a more humble background? Maybe a couple of professors for parents and Bunsen burners everywhere…?' Knowing that she sounded defensive, she added with a wry, humorous sigh, 'Believe me, I very firmly cracked the mould when I decided to do engineering at university and then, horror of horrors, put a career at the top of my to-do list.'

Mateo slid a curious glance across to the woman standing next to him. In heels, she was almost as tall as him.

Well, who would have thought…?

This was not the Maude Thornton he knew.

The Maude Thornton he knew was the archetypal, be-suited, impeccably but dully clad professional who did everything to an exceptionally high standard, but with her head down and in a way that attracted no attention to herself whatsoever.

He couldn't remember ever having had a conversation with her that hadn't focused on work.

She was exceptionally clever, highly creative, sharp as a tack and easily the most promising of the very bright intake working at his London branch.

She was a career woman with a glittering future ahead and that that was where his observations of her had begun and ended.

Until yesterday.

Until he'd glimpsed a side to her previously hidden from casual viewing. He'd seen her unflappable, professional demeanour suddenly morph into dismay and vulnerability. When she'd told him about her brother's party, and the fact that her plus-one had let her down, he'd glimpsed even more of that dismay and vulnerability.

And then he'd noticed a bit more.

Not just the height—that was something unavoidable. She was probably five-eleven, much taller than the small blondes he went for. No, he'd noticed the glossiness of her chestnut-brown hair scraped back into something contained. He'd noticed the blue of her eyes and the contrasting darkness of her eye lashes. He'd noticed the fullness of her mouth and he'd taken in the suggestion of ripe curves underneath the boxy skirt and loose blouse tucked into the waistband.

In the space of forty minutes, she had gone from the consummate professional—who had never, not once, roused his curiosity—to a living, breathing human being and he had responded in kind.

Why?

Mateo was at a loss to work that one out. Was it because her sudden burst of honesty had taken him off-guard and, in that fleeting moment, he had acted out of character?

Or had he, on the hoof, seen an unexpected opportunity for an arrangement that would serve both their purposes at a particular point in time? An arrangement that would cost nothing and have no consequences?

She wanted a plus-one to make an event she seemed to be dreading a little easier. He hadn't quite understood why she was dreading whatever party was lined up, but not his to question why.

And for him?

He'd thought of the thorny problem with his ex. Cassie had turned out to be the ex from hell. He'd broken up with her over two months ago, and since then she had developed a messianic zeal to cling on to him. She'd texted…she'd phoned…she'd started showing up at his home at random times with a list of so-called forgotten items she needed to collect from his penthouse apartment.

She had the tenacity of a barnacle and, whilst Maude had been contemplating the gloomy prospect of a pre-wedding party she didn't particularly want to attend, he had likewise been contemplating an equally gloomy scenario. Cassie had informed him that she would be popping over to get some shoes and a bracelet she needed and could he please be around to let her in.

Yes, he would. Because he felt guilty—that was the long and short of it. Guilty that he had taken his eye off the ball, guilty that he had been sucked in by a helpless fragility and a touching back story of having been bounced around between angry, divorced parents from the age of three. Not his back story, but there'd been enough misery there to match his own, and he'd fallen for it.

He'd fast discovered that her fragility had concealed a core of pure steel, but by then he'd somehow become her saviour, and she had refused to listen when he'd patiently explained that his qualifications to save anyone were sadly non-existent. He was no knight in shining armour.

Not only was it an almighty nuisance for him—and not only was it teeth-clenchingly frustrating to consider the prospect of having to set her straight in language she would be forced to understand—but he had one or two dark misgivings about whether he would be able to deter her in her desperate efforts to reignite what had turned to ashes.

He did, however, suspect that the one thing that might work would be if he were to become involved with someone else.

And over his dead body was he about to go down that road. After Cassie, a spate of celibacy felt like an extremely good idea.

But then…he'd gazed thoughtfully into blue, blue eyes and it had occurred to him that they could both do one another a favour. Truth would blend seamlessly into a tiny white lie and no one would ever be the wiser.

He would be Maude's plus-one and he would tell Cassie that he was involved with a woman. He knew that the mere fact that he was going to a wedding party with Maude, a party where family members would be present, would have the desired effect because that sort of thing was something he had adamantly refused to do in all the time he had spent with Cassie.

He had bought three cases of the best champagne on offer to take with him. He didn't think for a minute that his ex would think he was deceiving her and, if she did, then Mateo was confident that he could erase any such doubts from her head because, after all, truth was largely on his side.

'Can I ask you something?' Maude murmured, taking time out to have a private conversation with him before entering the fray.

'How did your…er…ex-girlfriend take the news?'

'About my new-found love interest?'

'Well…'

'No point skirting round with niceties.' Mateo's eyebrows shot up but his voice was thoughtful. 'Varying degrees of incredulity, fury and teary-eyed sorrow.'

'Poor girl.'

'Come again?'

'She was obviously in love with you.'

'Do I detect a hint of disapproval in your voice?'

'Not at all.'

'Is that diplomacy talking by any chance? Because, now that we're this week's hottest item, then it's fair to say we can dispense with the usual employer-employee, duty-bound responses…'

'It's none of my business.' Maude shrugged. 'As

we agreed, this arrangement…well…it suited us both. I suppose I feel sorry for her. Getting in too deep and then having to go through the trauma of being side-lined because you're no longer wanted.'

Maude thought of her own moment of disillusionment once upon a time.

She'd spent all her adolescent years with her head firmly screwed on. She'd come to terms with the fact that she was taller and bigger than all her friends… that she just wasn't the sort of girl to bring out the much-vaunted protective instinct in boys.

For a long time, she'd actually been taller than every single boy she knew and even after, when their growth spurts had kicked in, only some of them had caught up.

No, she'd dealt with her own gnawing insecurities under a glossy façade of indifference. She had listened to the ins and outs of her friends' teenage relationships and had never let slip any of the hurt that she was excluded from those youthful, heady first steps into love. Then she had hit university and within three months had fallen hopelessly in love with a guy on her course.

He'd been tall dark and handsome. He'd been someone who hadn't seemed daunted by her towering height and the fact that she wasn't model-thin. Maude had thrown herself headlong into a relationship that had lasted a handful of months, as unprotected as a tortoise shorn of its shell. With no teenage flirtations, no youthful broken heart, there'd been nothing to prepare her for the sudden storm of emotions or the crushing feeling of loss afterwards.

Small and blonde had won the day. The Perfect Guy had apologised profusely and dumped her for someone she could have popped in her pocket.

Since then?

She had been single minded. But she could still remember the hurt when that first tentative relationship had fallen apart around her ears, with all her deeply embedded insecurities about her looks crawling out of their hiding places, mocking her for being an idiot to have thought the cute guy could actually fall for her. Something inside her had broken and she'd known then that putting it back together would never happen. Her happy-ever-after would never involve all that starry-eyed nonsense about giving your emotions over to someone else's safekeeping, lock stock and smoking barrel.

Thank God the guy in question hadn't had to lie to her just to get rid of her! Maude cringed when she thought of what Mateo's ex had gone through, and some part of her wondered why the woman couldn't have read the writing on the wall from day one.

Mateo Moreno was a player.

Even if someone was buried under a mountain of books, and only surfaced now and again to take a breath of fresh air, they couldn't have missed the pictures in the tabloid press of the most eligible bachelor on the planet with some ridiculously beautiful blonde draped on his arm, gazing adoringly up at him.

Who in their right mind would ever get involved with a guy like that?

'You haven't met my ex. She's no shrinking violet,' Mateo murmured with wry amusement, and Maude looked at him, prepared to defend the female race from womanising men without a care for diplomacy. But he continued thoughtfully, 'I may have a reputation that precedes me, but believe me when I tell you that I never give any woman I date any promises I know aren't going to be fulfilled—and Cassie was no exception to that rule. Permanence? No. Not going to happen. Not in a month of Sundays. I lay my cards on the table from the start.'

'I'll bet that's a popular move with the ladies.'

'Where have you been hiding that sense of humour, Miss Thornton? I'm very happy you've decided to bring it out for some fresh air. Just for the record, I spoil the women I date—whatever they want, they get. Cassie, however...'

'Your ex?'

'Cassie wanted a whole lot more than that. She wanted the real deal, and my fault, but I should have backed off the minute I got a whiff of just how dependent she was going to be.'

'And why didn't you?'

He'd told her that she was funny...

Maude tried and failed to stifle the rush of pleasure that remark had given her. She turned to look at him and was entranced by his profile, by his dark, dangerous brand of beauty and by his casual indifference to it.

She blinked but discovered that it was harder than she'd thought to tear her eyes away.

He was compelling.

'I felt sorry for her,' Mateo surprised himself by confiding. 'She's a fragile person from a broken home and I foolishly ignored the warning bells when they started going off.'

'That's nothing to be ashamed of,' Maude countered gruffly. 'There's nothing wrong with empathy.'

'There's not a lot right with it when the outcome involves being stalked, and worse when the stalker risks her own mental health by not letting go.'

'What do you mean?'

'My amateur interpretation is that Cassie needs therapy. It's the only way she's going to solve ongoing issues, and that's exactly what I suggested, along with an offer to pay for the best money can buy.'

Maude was impressed. Something shifted under her feet. She was barely aware of it. No more was he 'just the boss' and even less just the cardboard cutout, one-dimensional womaniser.

'Being told that I'm involved with someone else will be step one towards her letting go.'

'Except you're not.'

'That's a technicality she'll never know about. That's why this arrangement is such a good idea. I get to set my ex on the right track and you get your plus-one whose role is to…what, exactly, Maude?

Pretend to be your boyfriend? That I understand. What I *don't* get is the *why*. Why do you need someone in this role?'

His voice was a low drawl, and Maude could feel his warm breath against her, because he had half-turned to face her.

She faced him and her mouth went dry.

The sounds of laughter and merriment faded, as did the spectacle of the marquee, the assembled party, the boys and girls weaving through with their huge, circular trays laden with delicacies...

Confused and alarmed, Maude sucked in a shaky breath and snatched at the self-control that had momentarily deserted her.

'I...it's always easier dealing with these sorts of things with someone at your side,' she stumbled.

'Still not really getting it. I can understand a large event where you don't know anyone. Could be a bit daunting, I imagine. But presumably you know most of the people here? And it *is* on home ground, after all.'

'I...'

Their eyes tangled and the breathless feeling was with her again.

'Yes?'

He leant into her and the hairs on the back of her neck stood on end as she did her utmost to wrest herself out of the shaky, sinking feeling trying to stage a takeover. He was so cool, so collected, asking questions that were only mildly curious...while she suddenly felt as though she were trying to balance one-legged on quicksand.

Was this what had propelled her into her initial foolhardy foray into confiding in him yesterday at the office—a sudden weakness when his attention was directed exclusively on her? When he asked her something personal while pinning her to the spot with those dark, brooding, mesmeric eyes?

'Angus was going to be my plus-one for the weekend,' she confessed a little breathlessly and then added, surprising herself, 'It's not that I'm anxious about being here, or nervous about having to socialise with all these people—I'm not. It's just that… I wanted to convince my mum that I'm not throwing my life away because I don't have anyone in my life at the moment.'

'Come again?'

Maude smiled sheepishly. 'Ever since I was a kid, my mother has been determined that I follow in her footsteps. She loves socialising and networking and having parties. She can honestly throw herself into the business of planning a dinner party with the attention to detail of someone running a military campaign.'

Mateo's lips twitched and Maude relaxed and grinned back at him.

'She wanted a "girly girl" and, well, what can I say? She got me.'

'I can tell you that *that's* the one thing you should *never* say,' Mateo murmured.

'My brother is six years younger than me,' Maude continued, staring off into the distance. 'And he's going to be married in six months. I'm thirty-two and my parents are still waiting for Mr Right to come along. My dad is okay with the road I've chosen to take, but my mum is convinced that I just won't find true happiness until I settle down. I think she's scared that I might end up on the shelf, gathering dust, because all the decent young men have been taken. So tonight...'

'Tonight you decided that a plus-one in this situation, with friends and family everywhere, would be just the trick.'

'Something like that. We should head down. I'll introduce you to everyone.'

'Before we go...'

He reached to stay her, his hand resting gently on her arm, and his touch sent a frisson of heat coursing through her body.

'Yes?' Out of the corner of her eye, she could spot her mother making a beeline for them.

'What exactly is the agenda here?'

'You... I've implied that we're an item.'

'And have you told your mother that you work in one of my companies?'

'I haven't told her anything. My theory was to keep it vague and play it by ear. She doesn't even know that my plus-one was called Angus. I just told her that, yes, I'd be bringing someone, but it was a new relationship so she wasn't allowed to pry. I thought that would do away with…you know…'

'Nosy questions about whether the time might be right for her to start thinking about hat-buying?'

'Something like that.' Maude smiled. He was a quick study.

'And they know that I'll only be sticking around for a handful of hours?'

'You're a very busy man. There's no chance you would be able to stay for the entire duration of the weekend. We can both make that clear from the start.'

'Must mean a lot to you,' Mateo murmured, 'Heading your mother off at the pass, if you're willing to go through all of this just to buy a little time.'

'You don't get it.'

'What? What don't I get?'

Maude turned to him and looked at him with clear-eyed honesty. 'I adore my mother, and I know she loves me dearly, but I've been a disappointment.' She blushed when he looked shocked, but it was the truth, a sadness she had never been able to completely bury. It was also something she had never said aloud to anyone. In a rush she continued, voice low, 'Nick, my brother, was always the one who slotted in easily—outgoing and sporty, and always with a string of girls phoning him up. Me? Not so much.'

Their eyes met and she said hurriedly, embarrassed at this rush of unwarranted truth-sharing. 'It's no big deal. This bash will probably wind up early, around ten, as some of us—my brother and his friends and Amy, his fiancée, and hers—are splitting and heading off in different directions. Nick and his lot are going to head to one of the bars to play snooker in a room they've reserved, and we're going to a club to fritter the rest of the night away.'

'And I will be...'

'Long gone—because you're a very busy man, like I said. Early mornings to get through emails and make...er...important calls.'

'On a Sunday? I risk sounding more of a crashing bore than a workaholic, with no choice but to abandon the love of his life in her hour of need...'

Maude glanced at his dark, amused face and thought that the last thing Mateo could ever be accused of being was a crashing bore.

'Anyway.' She quickly glanced away to where her mother was bearing down on them at speed. 'My mum's spotted us.' She plastered a smile on her face, and the smile broadened into genuine amusement when she took in Felicity Thornton's double-take as she closed in.

'Ah... I'm beginning to get the picture...' Mateo murmured.

Before he could expand on that, Felicity was with them, a force of nature, laughing and confident, giving her daughter a warm hug and openly inspecting Mateo, not caring one jot for politeness.

'Maude never told me that she was going out with

a hunk!' She burst out laughing and patted Maude's arm with warm approval.

'Mum!'

'Don't you *Mum* me, darling. Honestly…' She leaned towards Mateo and whispered, more than loud enough for Maude to hear, 'This daughter of mine is *such* a dark horse! But, no fear, you're here now…' Without standing on ceremony, she swept round to link her arm through Mateo's. 'And I intend to introduce you to *everyone*.'

She affectionately scolded her daughter. 'The time is over for you to be Little Miss Secretive! You're not keeping this dashing young man under wraps a minute longer!'

And Mateo allowed himself to be swept along, down the bank of shallow steps and away from the house, straight into the thick of things.

All the pieces of the jigsaw puzzle were beginning to fall into place. One glance at Maude's mother had answered a lot of questions. Maude had quite simply grown up somehow thinking that she was a disappointment because she wasn't like her mum—she towered over the tiny blonde.

The plus-one conundrum…why? Who would be desperate enough to entice someone into pretending to be their partner for a situation that should have been well within their comfort zone? That had puzzled him, to start with.

As Maude had explained uncomfortably, a thirty-two-year-old woman who needed to convince her parents that she wasn't about to end up gathering dust on a shelf, bereft of all options, as thirty-two turned into forty-two and then fifty-two...

Which still begged the question...why did a grown woman have to explain her choices to her parents? Why the need for approval? That was something Mateo genuinely didn't understand.

He had no parents. His mother had jumped ship when he'd been a baby, leaving him with his father. He had no memories of her whatsoever. He had no anecdotes about her at all. The only received information he had was that she had bailed for someone richer. She'd never looked back.

His father had done the best he could and, in return, he had gained his only son's fierce loyalty. There had not been much money to go round, but that had been fine, because impoverishment had been an excellent teacher. Mateo had learnt that the only thing that counted in life was hard cash, and his father had made sure to move mountains so that his son could get an education to give him a head start.

The worst time of his life had been when his father had died. Eighteen at the time, Mateo had hurt in places he hadn't thought possible. In the very moment of hurting, he had made his one and only mistake and had given his heart to a woman who had seemed so right at the time and had ended up proving so wrong.

Like his mother, she had not been bowled over by the proposition of having no money long-term, even though he'd told her that he was going to make it big. When someone with a bigger bank balance had blown in six months after they'd become lovers, temptation had proved irresistible. She had walked away and, if Mateo hadn't been hardened enough by lessons learnt in his childhood, that experience had hammered the final nail in the coffin of any lingering illusions he might have had about love.

Mateo thought he had consigned those memories to a safe place from which they could never escape, but for no reason, as he listened to Felicity chattering merrily next to him as he was absorbed into a crowd of family and friends on a balmy summer evening, they crawled out of their prison to show him all the things he had never had.

And that was when he really understood why Maude had wanted her plus-one. Not only was Felicity the polar opposite of Maude—diminutive, blonde, impeccably groomed and every inch the bubbly socialite—but it was clear that she absolutely adored her daughter, whatever concerns she might have about the path she had chosen.

He glimpsed the swirling complexities of an insecure Maude, raised in a middle-class background for a future she didn't want, defensive about the route she had chosen but compelled through love to try and please her mother. And, on this big occasion, the easiest way had been to conjure up a boyfriend that would make her parents happy.

She didn't want to disappoint. Next to her mother,

she felt ungainly, too tall, not polished enough…a disappointment. And Mateo felt an odd sense of pain on her behalf, which was ridiculous, but did make him realise that this arrangement wasn't quite as business-like a situation as perhaps either of them had imagined.

When he glanced at Maude by his side, reaching with nervous hands for a flute of champagne from a passing waitress, on impulse he reached out to link his fingers through hers, giving them a brief, reassuring squeeze while Felicity chattered away on the other side, dragging them along with breezy confidence to meet yet more of her friends.

'Don't worry,' he whispered to Maude with a smile in his voice. 'You wanted your plus-one? Trust me, you won't be disappointed…'

CHAPTER TWO

HE WAS HOLDING her hand.

Her ear tingled from where he had leant into her, whispering and reassuring. How had he known that she was nervous? He must have sensed something because, truthfully, she *was* nervous. Did the man have X-ray vision, enabling him to see what was going on in her head?

This was the first time she had ever brought anyone to her family home for an event like this, where so many family members and old friends were present. Sure, she'd had some passing dates in the past, and her parents had met one of them—a guy called Steve with whom she had had a half-hearted six-month fling until the whole thing had devolved into them being good friends.

But this? This was different and she *was* nervous. She was very much aware of the glances in their direction. Her mother was in her element. No guest was left unbothered. If there had been a Tannoy system in operation, Maude was convinced her mother would have used it to bulk-introduce him to everyone there in preparation for face-to-face meetings.

'Sorry,' she whispered, en route to yet another cluster of people—this time family from Yorkshire who had packed their bags and as they'd laughingly put it, headed off for 'those foreign shores called Down South' for the weekend.

'What are you apologising for?'

'I didn't expect all of this, and I don't suppose you did either.'

'All of what?'

'The attention.' She was on her fourth glass of champagne. Fortunately, food was also doing the rounds, soaking up the alcohol.

'What were you expecting when you arranged to bring the original plus-one?'

'Less of all of this,' Maude confided truthfully. She grinned and waved at some childhood friends, who made lots of gestures about wanting to meet her, whilst vigorously pointing at Mateo and mouthing questions.

'Why?'

The conversation was put on hold while the Yorkshire faction was introduced by a beaming Felicity. As the evening wore on, Maude was a little alarmed that Mateo seemed to be morphing from plus-one boyfriend to, 'Darling, is there another engagement on the cards?' boyfriend. She would patch that up later with her parents, make it clear to them that this was no more than a fling.

'Well?'

He had adroitly led them away from the pack towards a quiet corner of the garden and they now returned to the conversation they had earlier abandoned.

Food had been laid out on a succession of long, dressed tables in the marquee and a lot of people were inside as night fell and the summer heat faded. There was a small band playing in the marquee, easy-listening stuff guaranteed not to have the older contingent covering their ears and running for the hills.

Outside little groups had gathered, some sitting on the sofas on the broad patio. The fairy lights strung along the trees and foliage twinkled like little stars, mirroring the stars studding a velvet-black sky. Her mother had done a brilliant job of bringing their garden to life, turning it into a wondrous, magical backdrop for Nick's party. The food was amazing and the attention to detail was fantastic. If any of these guests weren't attending the actual ceremony, then they weren't going to be deprived of a similarly pleasing experience.

And Mateo…here with her… Maude was guiltily aware that she had enjoyed his presence way too much. For the first time in her life, she had dazzled, with him at her side. Her mother's eyes had shone with unabashed pride at her unexpected conquest. Yes, she had known with some unease that it was all a charade, and it was a charade that had a shelf life, but the temptation to relish it had been too much.

She looked at Mateo from under lowered lashes. So tall, so dark…so undeniably sexy…

She shivered, sipped from the flute and realised that it was empty.

'Why did you think it was going to be different?' he quizzed, and she shook herself back to reality and away from rampant female appreciation of his masculinity.

'Angus wouldn't have created quite the same… um…stir…'

'Poor Angus. Something of a bore?'

'He happens to be a very nice guy!'

'Damning words indeed. Can I ask you something?'

'What?' Maude narrowed suspicious eyes on him. He might have been by her side all evening, and holding her hand for most of that time much to her consternation, but they had had very little time on their own and personal interaction had been limited. This was the first time no one was around and the sudden intimacy of their surroundings made her shiver.

She nervously smoothed her dress and fiddled with the champagne flute, heartily wishing it contained some fortifying alcohol.

He was within touching distance. She looked at the brown column of his neck and hissed in a breath.

'I'm puzzled as to why you don't have a genuine partner to bring here.'

'Sorry?'

'You're a beautiful woman, Maude. So why isn't

there a suitable guy on your arm? Why do you have to audition for someone to fill the role so that you can keep your parents happy?'

'I...'

Mateo watched the play of emotion criss-cross her face and marvelled that he could ever have thought that she had only that one, business-like image she presented to the outside world. That was the image she had chosen to present, the highly professional career woman, but he felt as though he was seeing the real Maude for the first time, with all her hang-ups and doubts.

Or maybe that woman had always been there, lurking just beneath the surface.

He could remember a meeting some time ago, attended by various legal and technical bods there to cross and dot what needed to be crossed and dot-ted before the closure of an unusually big sign off. One of the guys had done his best to chat Maude up and Mateo had been amused at her body language. She'd posted so many *Do Not Trespass* signs around her that he'd been amazed at the guy's persistence.

Had the guy just not been her type?

At the time, Mateo had assumed so, but now he wondered...had she just not noticed?

Seeing her out of context here, he could see all those nuances that she had taken such care to keep hidden. For someone so confident on the work front, she was endearingly tentative elsewhere. Certainly she lacked the booming self-assurance that usually accompanied a comfortably off background.

'Broken heart?' he queried softly.

'What do you mean?'

'The lack of a man in your life.'

'That's none of your business!'

'Or maybe…' His voice lowered as he leant even closer towards her, and there was thread of lazy teasing in it that sent ripples of forbidden excitement racing up and down her spine. 'Maybe there *is* someone lurking in the background…'

'Someone lurking in the background?' Maude squeaked, genuinely confused at this tangent. 'What on earth are you talking about?'

'Undesirable…? Ex-con…? Married father of four…?' He did a casual sweep of his surroundings with his eyes and then lasered them right back to her flustered face. 'Coming from a middle-class background as you do, that's the sort of thing you might find handy to keep under wraps…although, as they say, the truth will out sooner or later.'

She blushed like a virgin. In the semi-darkness, he noted her nervous swallowing, her wide, alarmed eyes, her breasts heaving as though she'd run a marathon.

The dress was by no means revealing, and yet he was finding it very effective when it came to stirring his imagination.

What was happening here?

Accustomed to exercising complete control over

his responses to anyone and anything at all times, Mateo was disconcerted by his own wayward reaction.

Yet…wasn't there a novelty here that was oddly invigorating? When was the last time he'd been confronted by the unexpected? The tough bit of his life was over. The hunger and the searing ambition that had propelled him from nothing to everything had faded. He had the world at his fingertips now. Hardship had been the whip driving him forward and he had got everything he'd ever wanted—money, power…and everything that came with it.

Mateo had grown up witnessing his father in a never-ending cycle of trying to make ends meet. He had lacked a mother figure to put a perspective on things, to comfort him, because his father had never found anyone else. He was tough, had had to be, but on the way things had been sacrificed. He now had the world at his feet but this…this feeling of seeing things through different eyes…hadn't happened for a long, long time.

He was here for a couple of hours more. Why not relax and go with the flow until he left? He would never allow himself to get into any situation he couldn't control, so there was no need for any kind of alarm bells to start going off.

'Don't be ridiculous!'

'My sincere apologies if I've offended you.'

'Really?'

'Have I offended you?'

'You…you've jumped to all sort of ridiculous assumptions! Of course there's no one undesirable lurking in the background!'

'Perhaps you have no interest in men?'

'Yes, I happen to be *very* interested in men!' Maude spluttered. 'I don't have a boyfriend because…because…'

'Tell me. Why? I'm curious.'

'Because I'm not the sort that guys go for!'

Maude covered her mouth with her hand and looked at him with horror, because her own outburst had taken her by surprise.

Confession good for the soul? Since when? What had possessed her to say what she'd just said? It was something deep and fragile inside her that she'd always kept to herself, a little kernel of truth that lay at the very heart of her.

'What I mean…' She rushed into speech. Right then, if the ground had opened up beneath her feet, she would happily have helped matters along by jumping in. 'Is that I've always been quite a bookish sort and I've discovered, growing up…'

She licked her lips and dragged her eyes away from his dark, interested gaze to stare at something and nothing in the far corner of the garden, where the mellow lighting receded into darkness. Her heart was thumping hard and her mouth had gone dry. Her desperate attempts to explain what she'd just stupidly come out with tapered off into silence. Her eyes skittered across to his face to find him staring at her seriously.

The noise of everyone at the party having fun had receded. Of course, no one would question them being here, closeted away on their own because they were supposed to be a loved-up couple desperate for time out after hours of doing the rounds. Hopes of being saved by a nosy guest were therefore dashed before they'd even begun to take shape.

'Because you're too bookish?' Mateo queried quietly. 'Since when is intelligence a turn-off? Because you're tall? Many would find that striking. Maybe you've spent a lifetime living in your mother's shadow, but I don't get the impression that she would ever have made you feel so self-conscious that you ended up keeping men at arm's length.'

'I don't want to talk about this.'

'Why not?'

'Because none of this… This isn't *me*. I… I work for you…'

'Let's say that this is an unusual situation,' Mateo murmured, 'So the normal rules of engagement are put on hold.'

He was intrigued. He wanted to hear her story. It was unusual for him, because he was usually immune to back stories, or indeed any kind of touchy-feely stuff that could take him to places he had no interest in exploring. But he was finding that he just couldn't fight the curiosity tearing through him. In many ways, she was proving to be the most *natural* woman he had ever met.

Had he become jaded over the years?

He was thirty-six years old, but had years of being master of his universe, having whatever he wanted whenever he wanted, made him world weary?

With no one to answer to…no parents propelling him in any direction…had he become somehow adrift in an ivory tower of his own making, living a gilded life that was controlled and predictable to the point where nothing new was ever allowed to break through?

It was an uncomfortable thought which Mateo immediately shoved aside.

Self-control was the way you conquered the vagaries of life. That was something he'd accepted from a very young age and it had always served him in good stead. Naturally, he wasn't going to abandon it now because of an unexpected hiccup.

'I'm interested,' he urged in a roughened undertone.

'Do you ever give up?'

'That's not my profile, no.'

'Well…' One slip, Maude thought, and it felt as though a dam had burst inside her. 'My mum's a tough act to follow.' She smiled. 'You've met her. She's…she's always been the sort who sets a room alive the minute she walks in.'

'Maybe that's just the way you saw it when you were a kid and things have become stuck in that place.'

Maude shrugged. Was that what had happened? She had *always* known that her mother longed for a little girl she could dress up and Maude had not been that little girl. She'd been a tomboy as a kid and then, as a teenager, a bookworm who'd grown too tall and too buxom to fit into skimpy cropped tops and tight jeans.

Had she got stuck in a groove somewhere along the way, imagining that that was who she was when, in fact, that kid was long gone? Had she somehow rebelled against an image her mother had not actually been interested in perpetuating? Had her own lack of self-confidence made her overlook the very simple truth, which was that love was accepting and her mother loved her?

'Maybe.' She sighed. 'But I suppose I did feel… as though I didn't really fit in. Living in a goldfish bowl has its down sides and my life has always felt a bit like being in a goldfish bowl.'

She offered a tiny smile to detract from the sudden dive into seriousness. 'Anyway…' She threw a look over her shoulder. 'We should head back to the marquee. Part two of the evening is going to begin any minute now.'

She spun round on her heels but, before she could move away, Mateo had circled her arm with his hand, tugging her back to him.

'I meant what I said, Maude. You're a beautiful woman. Because you don't fit what you think is the mould doesn't mean you're not beautiful in your own right.'

'Thank you for that,' Maude said with sincerity. 'I know you mean well, but Mateo, what sort of women do *you* go for…?' She grinned when he flushed darkly and raked his fingers through his hair, and then she burst out laughing. 'I think I've proved my point,' she said drily.

Mateo watched as she began to walk away. He sprinted after her and caught up with her in a matter of strides.

'Wait,' he murmured. 'Is the love of my life now walking out on me? What's the world going to think?'

He slung his arm around her shoulder.

'Mateo…' Maude stopped abruptly and placed her hands palms-down against his chest. For a few seconds her mind went a complete blank at the sensation of hardness under her fingers, then she blinked and said crisply, 'No one's going to think anything. This is all make believe, remember?'

'Ah…but only the two of us know the truth.'

They were closer to the marquee and the scene of the action now. People were coming and going, the older ones on their way home, heading to the door to get their carriages, the younger ones already preparing for more of the same until the early hours of the morning. Someone called out to her but she was in the moment and didn't turn round.

'Which is that there's *no need* to pretend anything

when we're on our own.' Her skin tingled from where he had touched her. It had felt so stupidly natural just for a moment...so dangerously *good*.

The voice behind them got closer and then a smiling blonde was standing next to them, gathering a silk shawl over her shoulders on her way out while talking at the same time—rueful that she hadn't got to meet them properly, maybe another time, as Amy talked so much about Nick's fantastically clever sister...

She turned to Mateo.

'You don't remember me, do you?'

'Should I?'

He was frowning. For a few seconds, Maude wondered whether he was about to be accosted by an ex, but then the blonde introduced herself as, 'Georgie, one of Amy's friends from when she spent those six months in LA.' Her head tilted to one side, she said, 'We met ages ago at that art exhibition thing...you were going out with Cassie Fowler?'

Mateo smiled politely. It was obvious he had no inkling who the blonde was but good manners forced him to murmur something affirmative, at which the blonde burst out laughing.

'It's okay.' She winked at Maude. 'He'll keep you on your toes!' Then she turned back to Mateo to say with a hint of surprise, 'I had no idea you and Cassie weren't...going out.'

'We ended our relationship months ago.' Mateo's voice cooled and he glanced at his watch, an invisible signal that the conversation was terminated as far as he was concerned.

In fairness, the blonde laughed again and smiled with a touch of puzzlement, murmuring, 'Blow me, she never said...' And then she nodded goodbye and headed towards the bank of shallow steps leading up to the house.

'Well,' Mateo mused thoughtfully, 'That was unexpected.'

'I don't know quite a few of the younger crowd here,' Maude admitted. 'I've never met that girl in my life before. She'll be with Amy's party. Amy's a fashion journalist so they probably met through fashion. She seemed nice.'

Mateo shrugged and gazed down at the woman by his side.

'Penny for them.'

'Sorry?'

'You're lost in thought.'

'She's at the top of the steps with a few of Nick's pals and they're looking in this direction.' Maude sighed. 'She's probably wondering what the heck you supposedly see in me after Cassie... Wasn't Cassie a model? Look at me. I couldn't be a model if I spent the next decade on a two-hundred-calorie-a-day diet!'

'There you go again. Why don't we show them all and prove a point?'

He didn't give Maude time to object. He barely gave her time to think at all. He leant towards her, hand rising to cup the nape of her neck, gathering some of her long, thick hair between his fingers and tugging her close to him.

She wanted this. He could feel it in her tremble and the soft sigh that escaped her lips. And he wanted it too, more than he could have imagined possible. He'd wanted to touch her all evening. Only now, when he was actually touching her, did he realise that.

And it felt as if he wanted more…more than just a kiss. He wanted to silence her self-consciousness, make her know in her gut that she was as stunning as the rest of them. He wanted to make her feel really good about herself, as confident in her looks as she was in her professional abilities. Where was that urge coming from? For now, this was enough…

His mouth covered hers in a kiss that started gentle but then grew hungry, demanding, wanting more of the sweetness of her tongue against his.

The shooting hardness of his erection made him stifle a groan, but common sense wasn't making an appearance.

Not yet. He was lost and it was up to her to shakily pull back, eyes wide as she stared at him.

Maude could hardly think straight.

He'd kissed her!

Her mouth tingled. She wanted to trace her lips with her finger, but she kept her hands by her sides and somehow managed to weave a path through her confusion back to the reality of the situation.

Mateo had kissed her to prove a point. He'd felt sorry for her—wasn't that the truth of the matter? Confident in her work and clever at her job she might be, but she'd done what she always did when it came to that uncertain side of her—she'd laughed at herself, joked about the way she looked. And he'd automatically done the one thing that had occurred to him to do in front of an audience…he'd kissed her. Because he was a nice guy, underneath it all, and because he felt sorry for her. And, yes, because they were pretending to be an item and he'd been swept away by a bit of method acting because she'd pointed out their audience.

Maybe she'd given him some kind of invisible signal that she wanted him to kiss her.

Maude was mortified to think that.

'That wasn't necessary,' she said briskly. She wondered whether he could detect the slight wobble in her voice and hoped not. Her eyes were glued to his face, but in the darkness she couldn't begin to see what he was thinking.

Was he embarrassed that he had acted on impulse and done something he knew hadn't been necessary? Now he was staring at her—was he making comparisons between her and the supermodels he was fond of dating?

No. Maude knew in her heart that was an uncharitable accusation, but she didn't want to assume that he might have been attracted to her, even if it was for just a moment in time, caught up in the romance of a situation they had engineered. There lay a dangerous road—some gut instinct told her so.

'Not necessary,' he parroted huskily.

'No. Not at all. I mean, I know you kissed me to… to show them that we were really an item…but there was no need at all! I doubt they were even looking in this direction.'

'Is that what you think?'

'What do you mean?'

'You think I kissed you because I wanted to confirm the story we'd told everyone?'

'Y-yes…why else?' Maude stammered. 'Unless you felt sorry for me. I know I have a few hang-ups.'

'Shh.'

Maude trembled when he held one finger over her mouth as he continued to pin his dark, pensive gaze on her face.

'No,' she whispered, tugging aside his finger, but then keeping it linked with hers. 'This isn't me. I'm one hundred percent the professional.'

'Maybe I kissed you because I wanted to.'

'Of course you didn't. You're teasing me.'

'I never lie about things like this. I kissed you because you turn me on.'

The breath left Maude in a whoosh and the dangerous ground she feared trembled underneath her feet, like a sudden earthquake.

How was this possible? How could she turn him

on? Men ran to type, and his type was blonde and sensational. Was it because she was a novelty and, as they said, a change was as good as a rest? Had she awakened something in him, some kind of sexual curiosity, because he was seeing a different side to her, just as she was seeing a different side to him?

If that was the case, then the best and only thing she could do was to set him straight, because she wasn't born yesterday. The guy could have any woman he wanted with the crook of his finger. Very few would be able to resist. It wasn't simply because he was good-looking, or rich, or smart. Independently, those were traits that a lot of men possessed, and indeed some possessed a combination of all three, but not like Mateo Moreno.

Mateo Moreno was in a league of his own, and being swept up in the moment like an infatuated schoolgirl because he'd happened to pay her the compliment of the decade would be a big mistake.

'Do I turn you on?' he asked roughly, interrupting her thoughts with that single, devastating question.

'That…doesn't matter.'

'What do you mean?'

'It means that that's not what we're about.'

'Because I own the company you work in? Because I'm your boss?'

'Amongst other things,' Maude muttered, horribly uncomfortable but driven to stay and finish the conversation she had started.

'Believe me,' Mateo ground out with utter sincerity, 'I don't get it either. I have never believed in mixing business with pleasure. In fact, the opposite. I've always made sure to keep my private life out of the office.'

He raked his fingers through his hair and took a step back. The very fact that she felt the void and missed the heat of his proximity was enough to get the alarm bells sounding ever louder.

'But we're here,' she shot back urgently. 'It's out of the ordinary...*this*...and I guess it's taken us both unawares! It's been pretty stressful, having to keep up the charade. I didn't think... Well, you know, I didn't think that there would be this much attention directed at us, but maybe I should have known. We're both out of our comfort zones and we did something we would never have done in a million years!'

For a few seconds, Mateo didn't say anything.

She was flushed, her eyes bright. Frankly, she was desperate to shove this small indiscretion some place where it could never see the light of day again, and she was right. Everything she said made sense. They were both out of their comfort zones. With typical self-assurance, he had assumed that this brief adventure would be a situation over which he would have ultimate control, and why not? He had ultimate control over every aspect of his life, didn't he?

But he hadn't banked on the woman gazing earnestly up at him having so much sex appeal, nor had he catered for his legendary cool being sideswiped by feminine charms he hadn't come close to glimpsing in all the time they'd worked together.

Life, for once, had taken him utterly by surprise and he'd acted out of character.

This was the time to back away at speed—Mateo knew that. Maude Thornton wasn't like the women he was accustomed to dating. She was serious, about her work and about life in general. She wasn't someone to yelp with joy at the prospect of a fling with him and he wasn't the sort to declare intentions he knew would never materialise to get a woman into bed with him, however much he knew that she would enjoy every second of the experience as much as he would.

In every respect, they stood on opposite sides of a divide, and it was a very important divide. Forget about the fact that he was her boss—they were two consenting adults at the end of the day. No, this divide was a more fundamental one. This was a divide anchored in a difference of mind set, a difference of goals, hopes and expectations.

She expected love.

It was who she was.

She might have her personal insecurities, but she was a woman who wanted it all, or at least all the things he didn't want.

And she deserved to get everything she wanted without him messing with those dreams simply by taking her down a path she might end up regretting having taken.

'You're right,' he agreed. He glanced around him, suddenly restless and out of sorts.

'I know I am!'

'It's late. I should start thinking about heading back to London.'

'You should.'

He hesitated, shifted, glanced at her, looked away and then pinned his dark eyes on her face.

'You're…okay?'

'Why wouldn't I be?'

'You're right. What happened just then…should never have happened.'

'I hope the traffic back is okay.' She smiled a glassy smile and fiddled with her hair, which had unravelled over the course of the evening.

Mateo made an effort not to let his eyes drift down to her mouth…or dwell for too long on those chestnut tendrils of hair that had escaped the little chain of thin plaits forming a crown from which her long, wavy hair cascaded past her shoulders. He certainly didn't glance further down to the full breasts, more than a handful, or the slender waist curving out to rounded hips.

She was as cool as a cucumber while he…

Horny teenager sprang to mind. It was infuriating.

'Why don't you take next week off, Maude?'

'Whatever for?'

'Relax after the party. Surely you're due some time off?'

'Maybe next Monday,' Maude agreed thoughtfully. 'I can help Mum tidy up here and spend a bit of time with Amy. But I'll be in from Tuesday. I have a meeting with Doug Smith about the project we're working on at Canary Wharf.'

Back to business, Mateo thought, and it got on his nerves, because he was still in the grip of a physical response he had no time for. He tilted his head to one side and forced a grim smile.

'Have fun tonight.' He began to walk and she fell into step next to him.

'I'll do my best,' she said politely. 'Although, I quite fancy ditching it and going to bed instead.'

Mateo nearly groaned aloud at the image that suddenly flashed through his head.

'No need to see me to my car, Maude.'

'Okay.' She stopped abruptly. 'Safe drive back, Mateo. And thanks for this evening!'

Maude was held captive by the glitter in his eyes, the angled shadows of his handsome face.

That kiss still burnt her lips but it was something to be forgotten. They'd agreed.

She backed away then gave a small, stilted wave before spinning round on her heels and hurrying back to the house into which everyone had disappeared, no witnesses anywhere to their abrupt, detached parting.

The night air was still and humid, and for the life of her Maude couldn't work out why it suddenly felt as though the fairy dust had been blown away.

Maybe, just maybe, her mother had a point and she should start to think about finding Mr Right after all…

CHAPTER THREE

MAUDE SURFACED THE following morning to urgent knocking on the bedroom door.

It took time for her brain to engage and even longer for her body to follow suit.

What a night. There'd been too much of everything—nerves…tension…anxiety about playing a role to which she'd signed up on the spur of the moment, only to regret it when she'd stood in front of the mirror, looking at her reflection in a floaty blue dress that was so unlike the outfits her boss was accustomed to seeing her in. *What had she done?*

But of course, the second she had confirmed to her parents that Mateo would be coming, there had been no turning back. Had it been Angus, as originally planned, then it would have been fine. Angus she could have handled. Mateo, on the other hand, had kept her nerves in a state of high-wire tension so that, when she'd hit the club with Amy and her friends, the release of no longer having him at her side had catapulted her into just a little too much of everything—too much drink, too much loud music, too much dancing.

And too much of a raging headache at three in the morning when she'd just about managed to stagger to the bathroom and swallow a couple of tablets before crawling back into bed.

On the plus side, heading straight out to the club after Mateo went meant her parents had not had the opportunity to quiz her. Yet. Time wasn't on her side when it came to that thorny problem but Maude would cross that bridge when she came to it.

More immediately, the knocking on the bedroom door wasn't going away, and she eventually dragged herself out of bed, caught a glimpse of the time on her mobile and with a groan realised that it was after ten.

She flung on her dressing gown en route to the door, unlocked it and peered out, expecting to see her mother, bright-eyed, bushy-tailed and with a list of questions about Mateo filling a side of A4—none of which she felt equipped to answer when she was still nursing the remnants of her hangover.

She wasn't expecting Mateo.

In a rush, the dull hangover disappeared and she was suddenly as sharp as a tack, open-mouthed and stunned into shocked, disbelieving silence.

She was frazzled and bleary-eyed, her hair a tangled mess, while he looked as though he'd just stepped off the cover of a magazine. He was unfairly and sinfully sexy in black jeans, a faded grey polo and handmade loafers.

Maude yanked the bathrobe tightly around her and arched her eyebrows.

'What are you doing here?' Her mouth was dry and her crisp greeting emerged as a croak.

'You look lousy.'

'Thanks very much, which doesn't answer my question.'

'Can I come in?'

'No!' In case he had other thoughts on the matter, she inched the door shut a little more.

'You might want to rethink that, Maude.'

'Why? And you *still* haven't answered my question. You should be in London! When did you get here anyway?'

'Over an hour ago, to answer your last question first. Let me in.'

'Over an hour ago?'

Her heart was beating like a sledgehammer. She had no idea what was going on and the expression on his face was hardly reassuring.

'And before you ask,' Mateo continued in a low voice, 'I've been downstairs, chatting to your parents, having three cups of coffee and declining several offers of a full English breakfast. You really have to let me in, Maude. There's been…what shall I say…*an unexpected development.*'

Maude fell back. Her wide blue eyes were glued to his face as he brushed past her and strolled into the bedroom before swinging round, urging her to close the door behind them with a nod and a gesture.

She leaned against the closed door, folded her arms and stared at him.

'I'd sit if I were you,' Mateo drawled.

'You're panicking me. What's going on?'

'Before I launch into that, is there anything you want me to get for you?'

'Anything, like what?'

'Mug of strong, black coffee? Paracetamol? A glass of whisky, in case you want to try some hair of the dog? How much did you have to drink last night?'

'Not a huge amount—and I'm fine.' She'd subsided onto the chair by the bed and now stared at him in discouraging, stony silence. He was still standing in the middle of the room, elegant, sophisticated and utterly in control, whatever slice of bad news he happened to be bearing.

More than ever, Maude was conscious of her state of undress. Aside from knickers, she was naked under the thin bathrobe, and she was aware of the weight of her breasts and the push of her nipples against the abrasive towelling fabric of the robe.

They tingled, making her want to fidget.

'Just say what you have to say.' Her voice was gruff.

For the first time, Mateo looked uncomfortable. He sighed and moved to the bed to perch on the side so that they were on eye level, his thigh almost touching her knee.

'Where to begin? To cut a long story short, Maude, I woke up this morning to find a text from Cassie telling me that I might want to buy one of the Sunday rags because there was something about me in it.'

'You came all the way back here to tell me that?' She was genuinely confused. 'I don't understand. What would that have to do with me? Look, whatever went on between you and your ex is your business, Mateo. Yes, we embarked on this *arrangement* because it felt like it suited both of us, but I don't want to hear about what your girlfriend has to say about it.' Maude frowned. 'Why is that in a tabloid newspaper, anyway? I'm not getting any of this.'

'You also happen to feature in the article.'

'What do you mean?'

'I mean my ex has decided to have a little fun at my expense.' His voice was grim and his mouth had thinned, but his dark eyes remained fixed on her face, steady and grave.

'Explain,' Maude whispered, already predicting what he was about to say and dreading confirmation of her suspicions.

'The blonde who approached us yesterday clearly decided to find out first-hand what was going on, and she got in touch with Cassie to tell her about you.'

'She said that she didn't know the two of you had broken up...'

'I'd told Cassie that I was seeing someone but I never mentioned any names. Heck, Maude, it was just a piece of spectacular bad luck that someone at that wedding party knew my ex. Who the hell would have thought?'

'Amy knows anybody who's anybody in the world of fashion,' Maude said dully. 'That would have been the connection. What…what was in the paper, Mateo?'

'I debated bringing it, but in the end I thought better of it.'

'Why?'

'Because we're engaged.'

Maude's mouth fell open and she stared at him in utter shock.

'Sorry?'

'It would seem that I have found the love of my life with you and we're engaged.'

'No. No, no, no, no, *no*…'

'Believe me, I'm as horrified as you are by this development.'

'Have you spoken to her?'

'She's diplomatically not picking up,' he said drily. 'Although what would be the point of a conversation? She wanted to punish me for ending things and she chose the most effective way of doing it. I drove here at lightning speed on a damage-limitation mission.'

'My parents!' Maude squeaked.

'Thankfully, they don't subscribe to any Sunday tabloids, but they're going to hear the glad tidings sooner rather than later, I should imagine. I wanted to wait until we had this conversation before saying anything to either of them.'

'What…excuse did you give them for showing up at the crack of dawn?'

'Impulse decision to ditch the work commitments for the day.'

'I need to think and I need to get dressed.'

Maude realised that she was clutching the bath robe so tightly that her knuckles were white.

'We need to decide what we plan on doing before we go down,' Mateo said calmly, and Maude looked at him with disbelief.

'How can you be so…so…*cool* about this?' she cried.

'Would you rather I descend into screaming hysteria?'

'This is a catastrophe!'

'It's an inconvenience,' Mateo ground out in response. 'And one that will obviously be sorted, if not this instant, then certainly in the coming days.'

'And how do we set about doing that?' Maude demanded. She leapt to her feet but then remained rooted to the spot, glaring at him as the situation developed in her head in all its horrendous glory. 'You don't know my mum. This is what she's been waiting for…for *ever*! If we go down there and announce that we…that we're *engaged*…then it'll be all around her friendship group by this evening and there'll be an ad in the local newspaper by lunchtime tomorrow!'

'That's surely a bit of an exaggeration?'

'I'm thirty-two years old and she's been desperate for me to get married since I was in my early twenties.'

'You've really had to buck against the trend to develop your career, haven't you?' Mateo murmured, side-tracked by the image of a youthful Maude, digging her heels in and refusing to go down the prescribed route.

Strong, smart, feisty and a whole lot more.

He'd struggled to get where he was, had sacrificed a lot and had had to toughen up even more. They might have come from wildly different backgrounds, but in her own way she had faced her own struggles, and he admired her for that. That admiration was in his eyes as they briefly rested on her flushed face.

'Yes, I have!' Maude's head was all over the place. This was exactly what happened when she jumped in the deep end without doing her due diligence! It had all seemed so simple when they had thought up the idea. She'd been in a tizzy because Angus had let her down, and in Mateo had stepped with what had seemed a perfectly sensible solution. One that worked for both of them and would involve no more than a couple of hours with them both playing a part.

In some insane part of her she had actually thought that it might benefit her chances at branching out into more client-facing work if he got a chance to see her away from the confines of an office environment!

It had all seemed so straightforward.

It hadn't occurred to either of them that nothing in life was as easy as it seemed.

'Like I said, this will get sorted, but...' Mateo

frowned, thinking. 'It doesn't have to be the end of the world.'

'I'm going to change. You should go downstairs and…and…'

'Break the news that it was all a misunderstanding? That, in fact, we've never had a relationship? It was all a case of smoke and mirrors?'

'Well…'

'Isn't that going to lead to a flurry of questions? The main one being why you allowed everyone to think that we were an item in the first place?'

Maude hesitated. She tugged the robe tighter and glared. Shorn of the constraints of their normal working relationship, they were now two people, man and woman, without the divide of their established roles separating them.

It was just something else she had failed to predict.

His dark eyes roved over her, ponderous, lazy and doing all sorts of things to her body, making it respond in ways she didn't like and didn't trust.

She turned her back to him, rustled briefly in her chest of drawers, grabbing the first things that came to hand, and informed him with a toss of her head that she was going to shower and change and he was to wait for her downstairs.

She pulled on jeans and a tee-shirt. She would have to think about an outfit for lunch when she managed to get her head around what was going on.

She emerged from the bathroom to find Mateo

still in the bedroom and as relaxed as he could possibly be on the bed, half-lying down as though he hadn't a care in the world.

Before she could utter a word, he held up one hand and drawled, 'I have a suggestion.'

'You were going downstairs.'

'Incorrect,' he said gently. 'I was staying right here until we hashed this thing out.' He shrugged but there was amusement on his face as he held her gaze. 'I'm just far too much of a gentleman to contradict you when you ordered me to leave.'

'You're...you're *impossible*!' Maude snapped, moving towards the bed to stand at the bottom of it, arms folded. 'Okay. I have no idea what your suggestion is going to be, but I might as well hear it.'

Mateo crossed his legs loosely at the ankles. Maude, arms still folded, tried not to watch compulsively because the man was just so compelling, so charismatic, so ridiculously addictive to look at.

The jeans emphasised the length of his muscular legs, pulling taut across the thighs and riding low on his lean hips, and the polo had ridden up a bit. With not too much squinting, she could see a sliver of bronzed belly, and the sight made her feel all hot and bothered.

'By the way,' she snapped, 'Shoes aren't allowed on the bed. It's a house rule.'

'My apologies.'

She expected him to move and sit on the chair, which would have been a lot more calming on her fraying nerves. But instead he kicked off the loafers and they dropped to the ground, leaving the sight of bare feet, which was a thousand times more disconcerting.

'Think about it, Maude,' he said seriously. 'Your mother is fully engaged with your brother's up and coming wedding. She's put a huge amount of effort into making sure that everything is perfect.'

'She *has* been in her element,' Maude admitted.

'With the big day so close, would you want to ruin things for her now? And for your brother and his fiancée?'

'I beg your pardon? What on earth are you talking about? Why do you think I would want to *ruin* things?'

'If we go down and break the news that this was all a charade, then your parents are going to be shocked. Your mother…' Mateo paused. He thought of his own mother, missing in action. 'Your mother loves you, and for that you should count your blessings.'

'Why do you say that?'

'Because I never had one around to give a damn.'

The silence settled between them.

What the hell had possessed him to say that?

Mateo scowled. He waited for her to jump on his casual admission, to try and prise confidences from him that he had no intention of sharing, but she remained perfectly silent with her head tilted to one side and her cornflower-blue eyes, so calm and intelligent, holding his but without asking any questions.

He vacated the bed in one easy movement and strode towards the window to perch against the sill, arms folded, as were hers. He was filled with a sudden restlessness.

'My mother walked out on me and my father when I was a baby,' he said gruffly, still scowling, still completely bewildered by this departure from his normal behaviour.

'I'm sorry,' Maude said quietly.

'A better prospect rode into town and she decided to hitch her wagon to his and take off. She never looked back.' He raked his fingers through his hair and prowled the room, absently taking in the bits and pieces of Maude's past that were there in the framed photos and the children's books from a long time ago.

When he finally came to a stop, it was to stand in front of her, staring down and feeling a tug of *something* at the empathy in her eyes. He'd never in his entire life needed empathy from anyone, so why wasn't he turned off by what he saw now?

In fact, he'd never needed to talk about his past with anyone in his life before, so why now?

For a split second he felt vulnerable, and it was anathema to him.

'None of this matters.' He waved aside his momentary lapse with a dismissive gesture. 'You know what I'm getting at.'

'I do.' Maude sighed. She'd brushed her hair in the

bathroom but hadn't tied it back and it fell over her shoulders, halfway down her back. Distracted, she scooped it up, swung it over one shoulder and then toyed with the ends, chewing her lips, not looking at him but instead staring out of the window with a frown. It was another lovely day with the summer sun glinting on the huge gardens outside and streaming into the bedroom.

Mateo's startling admission had taken the wind from her sails. How she longed to ask more questions. She was in the grip of driving curiosity but there was no way she intended to breach boundaries. Enough had been breached already!

'I know it would stress Mum out…would stress both my parents out…if they were to think that we'd concocted the whole thing. You're right. There would be questions and all sorts of soul-searching.'

She made a decision. 'Perhaps it might be an idea to play along with the gossip. The wedding is in a matter of weeks. When you think about it, nothing really has to change. You disappear and, when I do come back here, I can always say that you're abroad.'

'The vanishing workaholic,' Mateo murmured.

'That's right. In the meantime, I'll get the opportunity to quietly start laying the foundations…'

'For our eventual parting of ways?'

'Relationships come and go.'

'Is that your experience?'

Maude frowned at the sudden change of subject.

How did he do that? How did he manage to take her down one road and then, when she was dutifully following him, swing down a side alley and lead her completely astray?

Maude hated that sort of thing. She liked to know where she stood. Growing up had been an insecure business, a balancing act between displaying the confidence she knew was expected of her while tackling the uncertainty of never quite fitting in. And then that painful episode at university, when she had foolishly given herself to a guy who had ended up rejecting her...

Over the years, she had got her act together. She was in charge of her life. Was that why she did what she did—a job driven by the precision of numbers and equations? When it came to structural engineering, there was no room for uncertainty or doubts. Either the maths worked and the structure was solid or it wasn't. She liked that. It was so different from the business of emotions and all the angst that came along with them. When she'd been studying design and the dynamics of concrete and timber, those days of being painfully shy—of growing up so much taller and bigger than everyone else, of avoiding parties because of the gnawing fear that she would be the wallflower glued to the side—had gone and were long ago and faraway.

'What do you mean?' Her voice cooled.

'Remember I asked you why you were still single at your age?'

'I'm not yet over the hill!'

'Remember I said that the reason I was puzzled was because you're a beautiful, intelligent woman? Did you get your fingers burnt in the past?'

'My private life is none of your business!'

'It is now that we're engaged.'

'We're *not* engaged!'

She glared at him and in return he slowly grinned back at her, his expression suddenly relaxed, amused and *boyishly* appealing.

'You're teasing me.'

'Partially,' Mateo admitted. 'Maybe I like the way you blush. Like you're doing right now. Really, though, we need to know a bit about one another if we're supposed to be a serious item. Your parents might think it odd if they ask a question only to find that we have completely different answers. They might also find it odd if I don't seem to know the slightest thing about your personal life.'

Maude hesitated. She'd embarked on this charade without thinking through the possible consequences and now, as she stared at him, she had a feeling of sinking further into quicksand.

Yet what he said made sense. He would have to know the bare bones about her and vice versa. In truth, she already knew the bare bones about *him*. He was a player who went for blondes and had made a fortune from ground zero.

And he was also a guy who had lost his mother... Who had grown up with all the insecurities of know-

*ing that he had been abandoned, whether he ever
admitted to those insecurities or not...*

Looking at her with brooding intensity, Mateo was
riveted by the expressions flitting across her face. He
knew that he was shamelessly fishing but he wanted
to know more about her and, if *he* was unrevealing,
then she wasn't too far behind.

What she gave away, she gave away without really
verbalising any of it in passing remarks...a look on
her face...the way she turned her head to the side,
shied away from whatever she didn't want to answer.

She wasn't interested in trying to garner his attention and so, rather than the usual coy remarks and
flirtatious, targeted innuendo, she preferred to say as
little as possible. And therein lay what, Mateo was
discovering, was an irresistible appeal.

'You must have had dozens of boyfriends in the
past,' he murmured encouragingly, and watched as
the blush deepened.

'I've been busy with trying to forge my career!'

'Too busy for...?'

'Okay, I've been out a few times, but nothing serious!'

'Ever?'

Maude shrugged, mouth set in a stubborn line,
and Mateo backed down, knowing full well that he
would pick up the thread of the conversation at a
later date.

'We should go down.' Maude interrupted the

stretching silence. 'Face the music. We can decide what happens next…well…maybe before you leave.'

'There's a big lunch, I hear?'

'It's the last thing I fancy.'

'Your parents can't wait. I suspect announcements might be made.'

Maude groaned aloud as yet more tangled, complicated strands wove in front of her, strands that would need unpicking just as soon as Nick and Amy were married off and her mother's attention was no longer focused on the big event.

'This feels like it's all getting out of control.' Maude looked at him with shooting despair.

She had gone to the door and was standing with her hand on the knob, watching as he slowly moved to join her.

'You're the inveterate bachelor,' she tacked on acidly. 'Your ex really knew how to interfere with the smooth running of your life.'

'Is there anything more dangerous than a woman scorned?' He was standing close to her, gazing down, and Maude was held captive by his eyes.

A frisson of *something* whispered through her and she stumbled a couple of inches back, heart picking up speed.

'I've never understood why a woman would want to get revenge if she's been dumped,' Maude mumbled. 'The best revenge you can ever get is by moving on with your life and showing the guy who dumped you that you really don't give a damn.'

'Is that right?' Mateo murmured.

Maude yanked open the door and stepped out into the corridor, which felt huge, light and airy after the enclosed intimacy of her bedroom.

She sucked in a deep breath and spun round on her heels, feeling his soft tread at her side and wondering what he was thinking.

She found out soon enough when he whispered into her ear, 'We have parts to play. I'll let you take the lead when it comes to being as vague or as graphic about the details of our searing, sudden love. Trust me, I'll be as curious as your parents to hear about how we fell deeply in love in the space of…how long? Not hours, I would suggest.'

Maude stopped abruptly, on the verge of reminding him that there was nothing funny about the situation. But before she could say anything he continued, his voice firm, inflexible and suddenly very serious.

'But, trust me when I tell you that I don't like this situation any more than you do. I also realise that I carry the full brunt of the blame for what's happened.'

'What are you talking about? We both entered into this…arrangement of our own free will.'

'I should have…' Mateo raked his fingers through his hair and skewered his eyes onto her, only the tic in his jaw giving away the fact that he was furious at what had happened out of the blue. 'Foreseen certain possible outcomes.'

'How on earth were you to predict that one of my brother's fiancée's friends would know your ex because she works in the fashion industry?' Maude sighed. 'I don't blame you. We overstepped, you know, boundary lines…and maybe that was the mistake we made.'

'And yet…' Mateo breathed '…what's the point of boundary lines if you can't occasionally step over them? I didn't get where I am today by obeying every single rule in the book.'

Maude shivered.

He was being honest. Mateo Moreno was the maverick whose genius had got him to the very top and mavericks had their own rule books.

'I'll try and be as vague as possible.' Her voice was a little shaky and this time it was because of the effect he was having on her, his proximity, his uncompromising masculinity and the way it made her feel—soft, fluttery and feminine in ways she had never felt before.

'If the tabloids have an angle on this, then the paparazzi won't be too far behind. I know how they operate. I also know how fast these stories die down.'

'Okay…'

'It would work for us to disappear for a few days. I have a place close to where I'm planning an ambitious project—a select housing development using the local natural resources and making every building as green as possible. It would be quite easy to take some time out there in the safe knowledge that prying eyes and wide-angled camera lenses won't be able to pay any unwelcome visits.'

'A place? An office? Is it the Scottish branch you're opening up, to explore expanding communities up there? Sounds perfect. We could work on whatever project this is in the meantime.' It sounded like manna from heaven to Maude—no conflicting emotions, back to an office environment where normality could be resumed. She could stay somewhere local, where no one knew who she was, and if Mateo said there would be no paparazzi, then there would be none.

She thought wistfully of an outpost in deepest Scotland where she could pick up being the woman she was and not the one who had suddenly decided to make a disruptive appearance in her well-ordered life.

'That's a really good idea.' Maude relaxed. Her parents could also be put on hold for a bit, as well as friends. By the time she returned to London the fuss would have died down and, as he said, they'd be yesterday's news. Gossip had a way of doing that.

They headed down to the kitchen, following the sound of voices.

Everyone was there—her parents, Nick and Amy and several family members who had stayed over.

The large kitchen, with its long, rectangular wooden table, bore the remnants of the full English

Mateo had earlier refused. Amy was by the sink, rubber gloves on, stacking the dishwasher.

As they entered, however, all heads swung in their direction. Catching her mother's eye, Maude wasn't surprised to see pleasure on her face mixed with bursting excitement and the gleaming look of someone with a million eager questions. Even her dad, normally the more sanguine of the two when it came to digging deep into her private life, looked thrilled to bits.

It was clear that the tabloid press had landed squarely in the lap of Amy and, sure enough, her mother's opening words were, 'Engaged! I *knew* it, my darling! What did I say to you, Richard? Didn't I say? A mother can tell! Oh, Mateo, you darling man! I'll bet you were horrified that whoever spilled the beans took the wind out of your sails! Were you going to surprise us with an announcement after the wedding was done and dusted?'

'You dark horse, Maude Thornton! You didn't breathe a *word* when we were out last night and we wanted to find out all about the dashing chap in your life! Now you'll have to confess all. Details, please, and spare me nothing!'

'Sorry, Mateo mate, you're going to have to get used to my wife-to-be telling it like it is. Congratulations, man!'

Champagne was brought out of the fridge and Maude let herself be swept along on a tide of good-will and questions, questions, questions. But she

could see light at the end of the tunnel and that for-
tified her. They would disappear on their work trip
to Scotland…and everything would be calmer when
she returned. So his hand casually draped over her
shoulders as she fielded the Spanish Inquisition, not
a problem.

And when eventually the questions slowed,
she tried not to beam as he said, ruefully, that he
wouldn't be making it to lunch.

He gave her shoulder a reassuring squeeze and
Maude already had her response on the tip of her
tongue when he continued smoothly, 'And you may
have to release this wonderful woman from her
lunchtime duties as well. The next few days might,
regrettably, require some Houdini escapology, so
we're going to disappear and miss the fun.

'By which I mean…' his audience was hooked
'…reporters standing outside houses making a nuisance of themselves. The quicker we leave, the better.'

Maude's ear tickled when he continued, his dark,
velvety voice as disconcerting as a physical caress,
'I hope your passport's in order?'

'Huh?'

Maude whipped round to gaze at him with genuine surprise.

'Your passport.' Mateo smiled and touched her
nose with the tip of his finger in a gesture which she
knew was designed to show just the right level of
loving affection. The guy could have won an Oscar.

'We're heading to my place in Italy!' He raised his flute in a toast and everyone else followed suit.

'Italy?' Maude parroted.

'I think you'll like it there, my darling. And key priority? Pack swimsuits. I'll make sure my private jet is ready and waiting for us by nine in the morning!'

CHAPTER FOUR

Maude discovered what it would feel like to be swept along on a rip tide.

One minute, she'd been bobbing along as comfortably as she could, given the circumstances, and the next minute…? Life was moving at warp speed and she was playing catch-up.

They had remained in the kitchen for another hour before everyone had started drifting off to get ready for the fancy lunch, which she would now not be attending. As soon as the last person had vacated the kitchen, she'd shut the door and spun round to face Mateo, hands on her hips,

'Passport? Swimsuits? Private jet?' She'd seethed as he'd calmly strolled to the fridge to help himself to some orange juice. 'You *told* me that we were going to *Scotland*!'

'Did I?'

'Don't you *dare* look at me as though I've suddenly taken leave of my senses!'

'If you recall, I didn't say a word about Scotland.

I admit, it would certainly fill the necessary criteria about being out of the way, but that office is far from finished and the development is still in the embryo stages. I think the locals might be a little alarmed if we were to show up with mock-ups of what their new housing might look like.'

'Very funny.'

She'd frowned and had had to concede that he hadn't confirmed where they would be going for their brief disappearing act. She had jumped to conclusions and he had cheerfully allowed her to.

With a thousand other questions to ask, Maude had found herself shuffled out of the kitchen without pinning him down on anything at all because, he'd pointed out, he would have to return to London to get various things sorted before they left.

'Time,' he'd said, 'Is of the essence.' This, as he'd been scribbling something on one of the paper napkins—the name of the airfield where she was to meet him.

'Don't worry,' he'd then reassured her. 'We *will* be working, and where we're going will be one-hundred-percent journalist-proof. There will be other people around, so don't be alarmed at the prospect of being secluded anywhere with me.'

'You still haven't told me where exactly we'll be going…' His words had gone some way to banking down her flights of fancy.

The truth was, she *had* catapulted herself into a state of panic at the thought of leaving the country

with Mateo. Swimsuits, private jets and passports…
they'd formed a picture of a holiday abroad and she
had reacted with instinctive horror.

Why?

Because he got to her in ways that sent alarm
bells ringing. Whatever simmering attraction that
had been there all along…whatever inappropriate
awareness of his sinfully potent good looks…had
been manageable in the contained environment of
an office, with the bustle of other people around, the
hum of computers and the buzz of phones. But take
that safety net away…

She had reacted with immediate horror.

She'd thought back to that kiss and had then pro-
jected to a few days spent lazing around somewhere
with a pool, and her nerves had gone into instant
freefall.

She was thirty-two years old! She wasn't a teenager swooning over the hottest boy in the class! She
knew better than to let her emotions rule her head
again. She was mortified because she knew that he
had no such qualms about being anywhere with her,
whether there were chaperones around or not.

Yes, he had told her that she was beautiful, but
Maude knew to take that compliment with a pinch
of salt. In the wake of her having confessed her insecurities to him, he had responded with kindness,
as many would in a similar situation.

Left with no option, Maude had decided that she

would simply have to accept the break with routine but treat it as work related.

And now she was here. At the designated airfield not a million miles away from where her parents lived, as it happened.

And their destination?

Italy.

She'd packed the minimum. He had sent a car for her and she had stepped into the sleek, black Range Rover, with its privacy glass and breathed a sigh of relief—because, as it had sped away, she had spotted two cars parked half on the grassy kerb outside the gates of the house.

Maude had had a comfortable life, but nothing had prepared her for the feeling of stepping out of that chauffeur-driven car to wait for a private jet to whisk her away.

The place was crowded. Small light-aircraft were lined up, booked for flying lessons. People were spilling out of the café, drinking coffee and gazing at the planes from behind a protective wire fence.

There were several private jets, and she was staring at them when she heard Mateo say, right next to her, 'I see you're travelling light. That's a first, in my experience, when it comes to a woman...'

Maude spun round, heart beating fast, and shielded her eyes from the glare of the sun.

He oozed sex appeal in a pair of faded jeans and a white, collared tee-shirt. At his feet was a well-used luxury leather holdall and he was wearing dark sunglasses, although he removed them to gaze down at her.

'I…just threw in a couple of things. We're not going to be there long. Your jet…'

'Will be here.' He glanced at his designer watch and then she followed his gaze to where a black speck was approaching the airfield, filling the air with the distinctive roar of its powerful engines. 'Right about now…'

Maude's mouth fell open.

The black beast dominated the airfield, a shark among minnows, and there wasn't a face in the crowd that didn't turn to stare.

'Come along.' Mateo jostled her briskly. 'I can't waste too much of this day. I have meetings lined up and I want you along for a couple of them.'

'Of course!' This was more like it—thank goodness. She would have to stop fretting about things that weren't going to happen.

Behind them, the driver had taken their bags. The crowd parted as they walked through to the jet. This was what immense wealth felt like, Maude acknowledged. Everything paled in comparison. It was the material manifestation of his ruthless drive towards the top.

He'd gone from an impoverished background to having everything at his fingertips. The ultimate maverick who had defied the odds to become the biggest lion in the jungle.

What had been sacrificed along the way?

Curiosity had no place here, but Maude was suddenly consumed with it. What had life been like for him? He had let slip that confidence about his mother…had shown her a glimpse of a boy who had grown up with the notion that he had been abandoned. Some things were very hard to paper over with common sense and grown-up logic—that was one of them. To think that you'd been left behind by your own mother, that she had chosen another life rather than the one with you in it, would have cut deep.

Was that why he was so detached from women? Why he could have countless relationships without ever allowing any of them to become a permanent feature in his life?

It was funny to think that, for all their backgrounds were so different, she too had absorbed things as a child that she had not been able to shake. She had had love and all the privileges of a middle-class background. Yet she had never been able to forget the way the other kids had looked at her when she had started shooting up—the giggles behind their hands, the invitations that hadn't dropped on the doormat.

She'd developed lots of coping mechanisms but had those experiences, like his, followed her into adulthood, defining what she did and how she reacted to stuff?

Had she spent a lifetime shying away from giving herself to anyone because of her own insecurities, which had been compounded by a youthful misjudgement with a guy, the sort of thing that happens to everyone at least once in their lifetime?

Of course she had. Maude knew that, just as she knew that time had gone by and the past should never dictate the present or, worse, the future. But what was to be done about it?

Her love life had frankly been non-existent for years. The occasional date, boyfriends here and there, had always taken second place to her career.

Had she been too scared to jump in at the deep end? Should she have done that ages ago? Maybe if she had taken a few risks, allowed herself to be hurt a couple of times, she would now be in a different place, emotionally less fragile. She wanted kids. She wanted a partner at her side. How long would she carry on searching for the one guy who wouldn't hurt her?

She surfaced from uncomfortable thoughts to find herself in the cabin of Mateo's private jet and she gasped and stood stock-still.

'Wow.'

'First time in a private jet?'

'No, I hop on these all the time when I have to travel short haul.'

Mateo burst out laughing. 'Why did I never see that sense of humour before? Help yourself to anything you want to eat or drink. I'm going to spend the time working.'

'You haven't told me much about where I'll be staying.'

'Haven't had the opportunity.' Mateo moved to one of the leather sofas, a pale-green affair that looked elegant enough for a five-star hotel, and Maude sat in a cream one opposite. 'And now...? Well, we'll be there very shortly. It's as safe as Fort Knox when it comes to ensuring privacy. I haven't had a chance to ask...but were discussions ongoing about this situation after I left?'

Maude sighed. 'It was all a bit of a rush, to be honest. Everyone was heading off to lunch, and of course, by the time they all returned, I was already back in London.'

'Good. Give it a few days and the fuss will have died down considerably.'

'Not with my parents. But when they next see me it will probably be the night before the wedding, and I can always make up some excuse for you not being around. It'll be hectic anyway. No one will have time to analyse why the guy I'm supposed to be engaged to has better things to do than to accompany me to my brother's wedding. And afterwards I can begin laying the foundations for it being a relationship that was never going to work.'

'You're very level-headed, aren't you?' Mateo murmured and she reddened.

'Yes, I am.' *Not his type*—that much she could tell from the amused expression on his face. 'Can I ask what the project is that we will be working on when we get to…er… Italy? How big is it?'

'All in due course, Maude. Why don't you try and relax for a couple of hours, instead of diving into work-related matters before we've even landed?'

It felt like a reprimand, a gentle, amused reprimand, and she nodded and looked away. She had come prepared for a reset. No more blushing Maude but back to the Maude he knew—composed and ready to pick up the baton with whatever work issue he threw at her. She'd even dressed the part, in a neat grey skirt, a white blouse and her flat pumps, no concession made for the heat, and certainly no hint that she might interpret this as anything but a necessary detour which would involve work.

She pursed her lips and made a show of looking around her whilst she felt like a fool. The space was compact but beautifully and lavishly furnished, with leather seating and small walnut tables dotted in convenient places for computers and drinks. A partition in the middle sectioned off a desk and chair and behind it Maude could glimpse a pale sofa that would double as a bed.

The pilot stopped by to chat for five minutes, and they were offered whatever they wanted by a young man smartly attired in blue and white, but largely they were left to their own devices.

Mateo submerged himself in work, oblivious to his surroundings as the jet took off…and Maude contemplated how the next few days were going to be spent.

* * *

It took Maude under a day and a half to realise that this was not going to be the working retreat she had originally hoped for.

They emerged after their luxurious flight to a rolling panorama of hills creeping up to sharply peaked mountains. She had expected the bustle of an airstrip somewhere, only to discover that the runway was actually on Mateo's own estate, which seemed to go on and on and on as far was the eye could see.

It was breathtaking.

He casually pointed out his acreage of vineyards stretching off into the distance and told her that the wine produced, fine though it was, was purely for local consumption—and of course his, whenever he found the time to return here.

She was led into an enormous villa, sepia-coloured and fronted by a sprawling, circular courtyard, which was dominated by a fountain.

Inside there was pale wood, pale marble and pale furnishings and, at the back, a splendid infinity pool. It was cleverly sunken into a carefully tended area that was contrived to look like a garden left to grow wild, from the dancing, coloured flowers to the artful planting of shady trees.

Of course, there were people around, staff to take care of everything, from the cooking to the cleaning. And in a building tucked to the side were offices where the people who ran the vineyards took care of business.

There were chaperones aplenty and yet, from the start, it didn't *feel* like work—not in these surroundings. Not with the sun pouring down like liquid honey on a lush, green, hilly vista.

Now Maude gazed from the window of her bedroom to the pool which she planned to avoid at all costs.

It was a little after six and she would be heading down shortly for drinks.

'Work talk again, I'm afraid,' Mateo had apologised. 'The project, as you saw from yesterday's drawings, will intersect the town close to the local church. We need to work on a way around that, making sure that every single thing is done harmoniously and is in keeping. Alberto Hussi is in charge and he'll be joining us for dinner.'

Maude's heart had lifted. *More work? In the most stunning place on the planet? Where lush, peaceful surroundings beckoned one to explore and relax? A place where computers should be hidden away and mobile phones stuck in drawers, out of sight? Perfect.*

There'd been no blushing when their eyes had tangled, his dark and unreadable. A crisp nod had said it all.

'And Maude,' he had added in a lazy drawl, 'I know that, now we're here, there's no game playing but there's really no need for you to dress formally.'

Standing out on the wide, marble-floored veranda that gave onto views of the open countryside, with nightfall throwing everything into dark relief and with the last of the guys from the vinery gone for the evening, Maude had shivered.

Behind them, two of the practically invisible members of staff were clearing away the vast array of wine glasses which had been used to taste various reds—two from Mateo's own estate, the rest from other vineries in the area. An elaborate meal had been served earlier in a formal dining room.

'I wasn't dressed formally. I didn't think so,' she had responded, and his eyebrows had shot up.

'Don't forget,' he'd murmured, the hairs on the back on her neck standing on end, 'That I know what you look like when you decide to do away with the starchy outfits. I know this isn't officially a *holiday*, and I realise that work is on the agenda, but you're in my home and I would like you to try and unwind as much as you can.'

The gauntlet had been thrown down.

Stiff and formal would signify that the problem was definitely on her side, that she couldn't relax around him…and, if that were the case, would he read anything into it?

Yes, he would. He would wonder why she was suddenly so skittish around him when she had been the ultimate professional in the past. And how long would it be before he concluded that he got under her skin because she was attracted to him? He was quite accustomed to those reactions from women, after all.

On the spot, Maude decided that she would ditch the three prissy skirts and the two loose, comfortable, buttoned-up blouses and resort to the culottes, khaki shorts and tee-shirts she had added to the pile on the spur of the moment.

Stepping out of her comfort zone, she resolved, would be good for her…

Mateo was waiting on the veranda for Maude to join him. He had forgotten how much he enjoyed the privacy of this sprawling villa, and the vineyard, which had been his life's ambition from when he'd been a kid. He came at the most a couple of times a year and never for longer than a weekend. He'd never brought a woman here. As he gazed over the dark shapes of the hills, and the marching silhouettes of the grape vines, he couldn't help but think how ironic it was that the first woman to come here was someone he was supposedly engaged to, to dodge the sort of tawdry publicity that would have prolonged a situation not of their making.

The breeze was cool. He could detect the rustle of trees, leaves and grapes swinging on vines. The smell was fragrant. How could he have forgotten what peace felt like? Naturally, there was work to be done here.

He hadn't been lying when he'd told Maude that it would be something of a busman's holiday. He and three high-profile businessmen with small but profitable vineyards were planning to expand into the community and breathe much-needed extra life into the area that had been good to them over the years. It had been something in the making for the past year and a half. This was a perfect opportunity to start the groundwork, but right now…?

He had the strangest urge to *play truant*.

He'd never had that urge. Even as a school boy, playing truant hadn't been on his radar. Playing truant was for losers whose life ambitions were no higher than the gutter.

For Mateo? He had always been far too driven and far too focused to go down that road. Even to contemplate it.

So why now?

Because his mind was preoccupied with other things… With a woman who had taken him by surprise and was now holding him captive to an attraction he couldn't seem to sideline…

It wasn't going to do.

He straightened as he heard the soft pad of her footsteps behind him, pausing by the bespoke glass doors that opened out concertina-style to the back veranda, a seamless divide between exterior and interior.

He turned around and hissed under his breath.

How the heck was a man supposed to concentrate on anything when he was confronted by a woman with those assets?

She was in pale-green loose culottes and a simple, white V-necked tee-shirt. But under those culottes he could define the length of her legs and, under that tee-shirt, the heavy swing of her generous breasts.

He lowered his eyes and moved towards her, aware of his body reacting against all the diktats of his brain.

'I hate to break the news,' he opened, reaching for a bottle of white from the silver wine-cooler on one of the many tables on the veranda. 'But Alberto isn't going to make it tonight. Problems with his mother. She's been taken to hospital with pains in her chest.'

'Oh, my. I'm sorry to hear that.'

'Wine?'

'A small glass, if we're going to be working…'

'Might be a bit of a stretch without his input, but of course. I see you've come equipped with your laptop.'

'Well, yes.'

'Sit, Maude.' There was only so long they could discuss work-related issues before the conversation dried up. He didn't want her to feel uncomfortable here. Whilst they had entered into this arrangement, having mutually agreed at the time that it was a good idea, it was his fault that they were now having to duck for cover from the slings and arrows his ex had decided to let loose. She didn't deserve to feel awkward or, worse, trapped into having to work because she didn't think she had a choice. She was in his villa, in his territory…the last thing he wanted her to think was that she was at his mercy.

'There's work to get through here.' He waited until she was sitting opposite him, then he leaned forward, his elbows resting on his thighs, his dark eyes serious. 'But, like I said, I want you to take time out and relax. The weather's good…whatever you want is on tap…' He slanted a slow smile at her. 'No one's going to be following us out here. I can show you the vineyard, take you to some of the local beauty spots…'

'You don't have to, Mateo.'

'I know.'

'I…it's…very beautiful here.' She reached for the glass of wine being offered and turned as a platter of canapés was placed on the table between them.

She made herself forget about the unnerving effect he had on her and gazed at the view.

'How long have you had this place? All this land… the vineyards…it's a world away from the rat race.'

'Yes. It is.'

'You sound surprised.' Maude sipped the wine and smiled.

'I'd forgotten how serene it is,' Mateo admitted.

He'd angled his chair so that they were both contemplating the same view, watching the same stars studded against the velvet darkness of the night skies.

A wave of utter peace crept into him, slow and steady, filling every part of him. For the first time, Mateo went with the flow and allowed himself to kick back.

'How often do you get to come here?' Maude murmured.

They both reached for a canapé from the table between them at the same time and their fingers touched.

He didn't pull away. Nor did he look at her. His hand lingered. Or was that her imagination?

The brush of his finger was as hot as the mark of a branding iron.

That dark, treacherous excitement she had felt before sizzled in her blood. She *wanted* to leave her hand right there, wanted the thrill of it touching his.

She had to force herself to bring the canapé to her mouth and then keep her hand on her lap as she continued to stare straight ahead, heart thudding in her chest.

'Not often enough.'

'Why not?'

'Work. Too much of it.'

'I suppose that's a blessing and a curse.' Maude smiled, darted her eyes across to his aquiline profile and shivered. 'If you don't work, how can you become…er…as wealthy as you have?'

'And is that where you're aiming to go?'

'What do you mean?'

'To the top…in pursuit of wealth?'

'Not at all.' She sipped the wine and let the alcohol loosen her. It was excellent wine. 'Money doesn't mean anything to me.'

'That's because you've always had access to it.' Mateo glanced at his glass to see that it was finished so he helped himself to another and topped up Maude's as well.

He found himself thinking about his childhood, the road he never went down, and knew that the last thing he wanted to do was go there in yet more confessional mode.

'Maybe. Probably. It would have been a lot easier to have become a spoiled brat.'

Mateo grinned, admiring her honesty. He looked at her and, when their eyes met, he held her gaze.

'I've met a lot of those in my life,' he said huskily.

'Trust me. So have I. Why here? Can I ask?'

'What do you mean?'

'Why do you have a house here? In this particular place in Italy? Is this where you grew up?'

And, just like that, Mateo knew that he was going to do the unthinkable and lower his defences. Something about being here, perhaps, with the silence around them and the memories this place stirred… *and being in this place with this particular woman.*

She was so measured, so intelligent…so unlike the women he went out with.

He brushed aside the whisper of what a threat might feel like, because it was only what he didn't know that might prove dangerous. Everything else—people, women, business—you were in control of, once you knew what you were dealing with. And, despite surprises along the way, Mateo knew Maude. There might be many sides to her he hadn't seen before but that was true of everyone. The fact was, she remained his cool-headed, dependable employee—serious and dedicated, risk-averse and sensible.

She couldn't have been more different from Cassie. She wanted nothing from him and was sharp and insightful enough to know that, as two human beings went, they were worlds apart, whatever heat had burned between them when they had kissed.

'Not a million miles away,' Mateo confessed. 'My father worked at a vineyard. Not one of these local ones, but a bigger, more commercial concern. He was housed there. He never owned his own place because he was never paid enough.'

'Did that bother you?' Maude asked curiously.

'It made me realise,' Mateo said drily, 'That, when I got older, the only vineyard I would ever stay on would be one I owned.'

'And you did it.'

Mateo looked around him, the master of all he surveyed. He'd put in the blood, sweat and tears and he'd done it. This vineyard was his crowning glory even though he had many other properties and holdings all over the world.

So how was it that he so seldom made it over here?

This place was in his blood.

'Food beckons.' He stood up and then turned to look at Maude as she hurriedly scrambled to her feet.

He reached out, an automatic gesture to help her up, and she linked her fingers tightly with his as he pulled her up towards him so that she stumbled forward into him and against him, hard chest against the soft swell of her breasts...

Mateo's breath caught sharply in his throat. His body fought against his brain and he heard his own raspy breath as the heat poured through him, staying his hand on hers and keeping her against him.

He was only inches away from kissing her.

'My apologies.' Mateo barely recognised his own voice because it was so unsteady.

'What are you apologising for?'

'You really want to know?'

Maude knew. He could see her body trembling with knowing. *Temptation*. She'd seen it in the dark flare in his eyes and felt it in the heat from his body that matched hers. But he was sensible enough to know that, alone out here, they should fight the temptation. There was no one looking this time, demanding a kiss to prove a non-existent relationship.

There was just the two of them, and no…

They couldn't let themselves be swept away by this. Could they? Could she? She'd been swept away once by a guy she'd thought was right for her. It would be crazy to let herself be swept away by a guy who was so, so wrong for her in every way...wouldn't it?

She stepped back but her eyes were still held captive by his.

'Dinner,' she croaked. 'We should go in.'

Their eyes held for a few seconds and then he nodded, raked his fingers through his hair and did her a favour by not saying anything at all. Because she had no idea what she would have done if he'd actually come right out and dealt with the elephant in the room.

CHAPTER FIVE

MAUDE WAS ASTOUNDED at how easy it was to forget about London, her parents, her brother's imminent wedding and a phoney engagement story doing the rounds courtesy of Mateo's spiteful ex.

The truth was he could not have brought her to a more perfect spot when it came to escaping those thorny problems. His beautiful villa, with its stretching vistas of rolling hills and trellises heavy with grapes disappearing into the horizon, was so wonderfully peaceful that it was hardly surprising that her brain was finding it very easy to shut down.

It was also making Maude realise just how little time she had ever taken to really unwind. She had spent so many years keen to prove that she could pursue the career she wanted and be happy that most of her time was devoted to work.

Her degree had been enormously difficult, and afterwards she had launched herself into the job market without pausing for breath. While friends had taken a year out to travel or pick up casual work in new cities, she had been filling out online application forms for jobs and, once she had landed her first job, she had had no time to surface.

Total peace would have been achieved now had she not been so acutely aware of Mateo and the disturbing effect he had on her. For the past two days they had circled one another, making no mention of those fraught few moments when the world seemed to have stood still and she had had to fight off the yearning to drown in the temptation of touching him.

She'd pulled back. He'd pulled back. Common sense had been reinstated...

And since then work had continued, interrupted by a trip to three of the local towns, where she had wandered around on her own, dazzled by a scenery of jumbled sepia houses clambering up hills, nestled amidst lush greenery. Mateo, on one occasion, had joined her, taking her to a quaint antiques market and an ancient church, its walls decorated with Mediaeval and Renaissance art.

He had been informative, knowledgeable, charming and very, very polite, and Maude had hated it.

How on earth could she *miss* the treacherous excitement of the forbidden? She just *did*. He had awakened something in her and she was helpless to fight it.

Clearly, he had no such problem. Maybe he had sensed the attraction and was now in a hurry to ensure it came to nothing.

For the past two evenings, there had been company, one or other of his associates from the nearby estates, and as soon as they had gone he had excused himself and disappeared into the bowels of the villa to work.

Where was he now at a little after five in the afternoon? Giving her time to relax, he had said first thing that morning, over a breakfast of fresh breads served on the veranda by Luisa, the young girl who was the resident chef.

'I won't be back until reasonably late,' he had apologised, glancing at his watch and rising to his feet, his body language letting her know that he was a guy who didn't have time to hang around chatting. 'But you can instruct the chef to prepare whatever you want for yourself this evening.'

He'd dispensed politeness and she'd responded in kind, murmuring something and nothing about a salad, while her eyes had skittered away from the temptation to drink him in. He was so dark, virile and stupidly sexy in a pair of cream chinos and a white linen shirt cuffed to the elbows and hanging over the waistband of the trousers. He should have looked sloppy but instead he looked way too hot for her peace of mind.

She should have been grateful for the brief reprieve from being in his company but instead, as she'd heard the purr of his sports car leaving, she'd felt a surge of silly disappointment which she'd had to squash by bracingly telling herself that the less she saw of him, the better.

...ing, she would ask him about leav-
...when?

...as something they hadn't discussed. He'd be-
...e submerged in work and she had fallen in step,
working alongside him with the ease of familiarity,
and enjoying the vision he was creating with the
other vineyard owners for some of the tiny villages
they did a lot to support.

On one occasion, she had met some of the people who had jobs in the various wineries. A spread
had been laid out under an awning in the centre of
one of the villages, in a square surrounded by old
stone buildings with a tiny, well used church in the
corner. Maude had become consumed by the sort of
community spirit that was very hard to find in London. The sun had poured down from a milky blue
sky and, intrigued, she had seen a different Mateo,
a more relaxed Mateo, one who listened to everything the locals were saying and who communicated
with them with curiosity and interest, keen to hear
what had been going on. She had smiled when he
had apologised for having stayed away for far too
long, his Italian fast and his gestures so typically,
exotically foreign.

Meanwhile, her mother had texted daily, filling
her in on progress with the wedding and keeping a
dignified and tactful silence on the subject of the engagement. Although, the day after they had arrived
in Tuscany, she had confessed that she had got hold
of the tabloid where the gossip had first hit the press

and just couldn't help being thrilled that her baby had finally found the man of her dreams.

And who could blame her? Because Mateo was a dream.

Maude fretted over what the next step in their ill-judged charade would be but, oh, how easy it was to put those niggling anxieties on hold over here.

How easy to live in this parallel universe, where life had taken on a technicolour clarity, and every minute was spent in a state of illicit heightened excitement.

And the surroundings... They were like nothing she had ever experienced, a world apart from middle class suburbia, which looked mundane in comparison.

Maude paused where she was for a few seconds and breathed it all in. For the first time, she was going to use the swimming pool. Mateo wasn't going to be around, and she had told Luisa that she could head off early, as there would be no need to prepare an evening meal. After a lot of gesticulating, she had also managed to communicate to the smiling Italian *nonna* who was the daily help that she too could leave ahead of schedule.

It was slightly cooler now but still very warm and the sky was a watercolour blend of deep blues, light blues and tinges of streaky orange.

In the distance, the hills were vague shapes cutting across the horizon, framing the rustle of green that fanned out in waves across the acres of Mateo's estate.

The pool looked amazing and Maude walked towards it, not bothering to test the water or let her body adjust to the cold. She tossed her towel on one of the wooden loungers, along with the bag she had brought containing her sun block, her shades and a book she was having trouble finishing and dived in.

She was a strong swimmer. She had always loved the way she could hear herself really think when she was under water. She had no idea how many lengths she was doing. She picked up speed, slicing through the crisp, cold water, her body remembering all the flips and turns from way back when.

She was clearing her eyes, surfacing at the deep end, ready to do a few more laps before calling it a day, when she realised that she was no longer alone at the pool.

She swiped wet hair from her face and saw his feet first.

No shoes, just brown ankles… As she raised her eyes, she saw lean, muscular calves…up and up to his thighs…and then a pair of black swimming trunks.

She was getting a little breathless from treading water in the deep end but there was no way she was going to heave herself out in front of him.

'Are you coming out?'

Maude gazed up and her mouth dried at the sight of his bare torso. He had a white towel slung over his shoulders and he was staring down at her through dark, reflective sunglasses.

On every level, Maude felt disadvantaged.

'Give me your hand. I'll help you out.'

'I was about to swim a few more lengths, as it happens. What are you doing here? I didn't think you were going to be back until…er…much later.'

'Disappointed?'

'This is your house!' Her voice rose an octave higher. 'You can come and go as you please!'

'Many thanks for that.' He grinned, slid the towel off and tossed it onto the nearest sun lounger. 'The pool was beckoning. It's not often it gets used and I decided it would be more fun to test the water than sit through another meeting that can wait until tomorrow. Mind if I join you?'

'Your house! Your pool!' Her voice was squeaky and high, and she was bright-red and uber-conscious of her body on show, distorted in size because of the water.

In an embarrassed rush, she struck out, swimming fast to the opposite end of the pool and then resting on the steps with the sun on her shoulders, watching as he slid into the water to swim lazily towards her, with perfectly modulated strokes.

As he closed the distance between them, more and more her stomach tightened into panicked knots.

The muscles rippled in his broad shoulders. It was a fascinating sight.

Her breathing slowed as he joined her on the steps,

lying back on his elbows for a few seconds, eyes closed to the sun.

They flew open when he turned to face her and Maude hurriedly looked away.

'How long have you been out here?'

'Forty minutes or so.'

'It's nice to see you relaxing, Maude. You've been working a lot while you've been here.'

'Wasn't that part of the deal?'

'Was it?'

'Of course it was,' she confirmed stoutly, still staring straight ahead, glassy-eyed and uber-conscious of him so close to her and of the water lapping around them.

She tried not to look at herself.

She could feel all her hang-ups about her appearance waiting in the wings, and that was the last thing she needed.

'I thought the deal was basically to clear off for a few days until the fuss died down and, coincidentally, there was work that could be done over here.'

'Which reminds me, I've been meaning to ask— how much longer do you think we should stay here? Amy's been keeping her ear to the ground, and there's lots of gossip in certain circles, but I can handle that if you can. I mean, I would rather not have people coming at me with cameras, but I expect that'll have disappeared by the time we get back to London.'

'There's a celebrity marathon for charity happening next week,' Mateo told her. 'Once that hits the streets of London, all cameras will have moved in that direction.'

'I'd forgotten about that. I'm surprised you take an interest.'

'I was invited to the big opening event.' He shrugged. 'Not my thing. At any rate, I propose we stay out here for another week. A celebrity marathon is one hundred percent guaranteed to throw up a lot more fodder for the rumour mill. That aside, the work out here can be finished in another week, with sufficient instructions in place and signatures on dotted lines for work to begin.' He turned to her and grinned. 'It's not that much of a hardship being here, is it, for a few more days?'

'No, of course not.' Maude could feel his eyes on her. He was close enough for her to feel his warm breath on her cheek as well. Both were horribly disconcerting. 'I just thought that you...well...might want to get back to work.'

'Like I said... I'm working here.'

'Yes, I get that.'

'If you want the truth, I'm finding it oddly relaxing being here. It's been a while.'

Maude shifted and looked at him, and he turned and looked right back at her.

He had ditched the sunglasses and she could see sincerity in his eyes mingled with that most human of traits: hesitation.

Why did she feel so comfortable with this man?

Why did she lecture herself about being professional around him only to jettison her fine intentions the minute he got close?

He made her weak and she hated it.

Yet she found herself saying, 'I've wondered about that.'

'Have you, now?'

'It's not my business…'

'Despite the fact that we're engaged?'

Maude went bright-red but held her ground, ignoring his gentle teasing. 'Why would you have this wonderful place out here…all these acres of vineyard…and then delegate it to other people to run so that you can spend time holed up in cold, busy, grey London?'

'There's money to be made holed up in cold, busy, grey London.' Mateo relaxed back. 'I like your choice of wording, Maude. Very evocative. I've never thought of living in London on a par with being in a prison cell.'

'You know what I mean.' But she was smiling, enjoying this return to cordiality, and realising just how much she had disliked the abrupt remoteness between them earlier.

'I do, as it happens. But I meant it. These vineyards… Yes, they're profitable, but they're a hobby. A sentimental hobby. My only one. However, it's not real life being out here, and I can't afford the time to laze around for weeks on end watching the grapes swell and grow.'

'It sounds pretty perfect to me.' Maude heard herself sigh.

She shook herself and sat forward. The sun was beginning to fade.

'I'm sorry, but I had no idea you were going to be back, so I sent the ladies home. I just fancied something light for dinner and I didn't want anyone fussing around.'

'Excellent plan!'

'A couple more laps and then we go in?'

He didn't reply, instead propelling himself forward to slice through the water, making light work of one length and then effortlessly turning around to swim back.

Maude was spellbound by the power and the speed.

She'd always fancied herself an excellent swimmer but, when she pushed off to join him for some remaining laps, she found that it was a struggle to keep up when he seemed to be doing no more than barely breaking sweat.

She'd forgotten all about her inhibitions and self-consciousness when, fifteen minutes later, she stepped out of the pool at the shallow end to fetch her towel from the deck chair.

Mateo, reaching for his own towel to sling around his waist, stopped dead in his tracks and stared.

She was all woman.

He'd always gone for slender little blondes. He now had no idea why when an earthy, rounded, well-built brunette was doing all sorts of crazy things to his body.

He felt the heat of an erection and he immediately made sure the towel was very securely fastened around his waist. Too much more of an eyeful and God only knew what might push up against it, embarrassing them both.

He flushed when she turned to him to ask, innocently, 'Where did you learn to swim like that? You're amazing.'

For a few seconds Mateo was deprived of speech. She was drying her hair, body tilted, her heavy breasts practically spilling out of the very sober, very old-fashioned one-piece swimsuit. She stood at nearly six feet and her legs were long and well-shaped, her hips rounded and feminine, dipping to a narrow waist, and he could see her way-more-than-a-handful breasts. It was sheer torture, not giving in to the urge to stare like a teenage boy with no self-restraint.

He looked away hurriedly and began strolling towards the house. He breathed more easily when she fell into step alongside him—just about.

'Self-taught,' Mateo said in a roughened undertone. He cleared his throat. This was about as *un*cool as he had ever felt in his life.

'Wow. I'm impressed! I had tons of lessons growing up and I always thought I was pretty decent. I used to out-swim the boys in my class most of the time, but I'm green round the ears compared to you!'

They were back in the villa, front door closed and the pale marble flooring generating wonderful cool. He turned to her, still fighting his own rebellious body, knowing that it was imperative to keep some distance at the moment or else make a fool of himself by gawking. Damn it, he wished she would just *cover up*. How much more could a red-blooded male deal with?

'You barely looked as though you...'

'I'm going to head upstairs, Maude. Also, I have work to catch up on—emails. Probably a good idea for you to carry on without me this evening as planned.'

'Oh, yes, of course...'

'Right.' Mateo took a couple of steps back. 'I'll head up now. I will see you in the morning.'

He swung round on his heels and Maude watched him vanish into the bowels of his mansion with a sinking heart. What on earth had possessed her to start feeling as though they were best friends, relaxed, chatting and swimming in his pool without a care in the world...*as though they really were the couple they were pretending to be?*

Mortified, she raced up to her bedroom, towel clutched tightly around her, locked the bedroom door and leant against it, calming down.

Her bedroom was more of a suite, with a seating area and a giant *en suite*. Pale wood made the floors underfoot cool, as did the overhead ceiling fan which she immediately turned on, finding the whirr of the blades soothing.

She forced herself to have a long bath and to relax but, by the time she made it to the kitchen an hour and a half later, she had determined that hanging around for another week or so, until reporters might or might not have lost interest in their stupid phoney engagement, wasn't going to do.

Indeed, there was no reason for her to stay on at all. Yes, she was sure he had work to do out here, and it was convenient being around to get through it, but what did that have to do with her? She wasn't needed for consultation on any of the engineering issues because they had their own guy out here who had covered all of that.

She could return to England, go and stay with her parents and there she could start laying the groundwork for the house of cards that would come tumbling down approximately one day after Nick and Amy were safely married off and her parents' attention was no longer focused on the wedding.

And if there were reporters lurking behind bushes? They would soon lose interest when they clocked that there would be no pictures of the loved-up couple, but just of her. And if they wanted to ask intrusive questions then she was fully capable of smiling, nodding and saying absolutely nothing at all.

She would also take a couple of weeks off, which she was entitled to. At the end of it, and by the time she finally clapped eyes on Mateo again, she would hopefully have rid herself of her inconvenient attraction.

After all the formal evening meals prepared by a qualified chef, it was fun rooting through the fridge and larder for bits and pieces with which make herself something to eat.

She had washed her hair but not bothered to dry it and she knew that it would get very curly as it dried. On her own, and with no need to dress to impress, she was in cut-off jeans, a tee-shirt and some flip-flops. She had brought down her mobile and was playing some music, half-humming along even though the audio was poor, so only became aware of Mateo's looming presence when she swung round with a plate of salad in one hand and a glass of wine in the other.

She had no idea how she retained a grip on both as she stopped dead in her tracks to stare at him, utterly confounded by his unexpected appearance.

He had vanished earlier, leaving her with the impression that she was the last person he wanted to spend time with. He had shut down her friendly chit chat in mid-flow and stalked off without a backward glance, leaving her to assume that he was bored with her company and keen for her to realise that he wasn't her pal, let alone anything else. Possibly just in case she started getting ideas.

Yet here he was, and Maude could feel a sense of fury building because him just standing there, darkly, dangerously and thrillingly sexy was scuppering all her carefully worked out plans.

'I thought you were working,' she said tightly. She galvanised her body into motion, walked towards the kitchen table and sat down with her plate and glass of wine. She didn't look at him. This was his house, and she could hardly stop the man from moving freely inside it, but her heart was thumping and she could feel her resentment ratcheting up.

'I couldn't.'

Maude shrugged, eyes fixed on her plate as she dug into the salad which tasted of cardboard.

She switched the music off and then wished she hadn't because the sudden silence was now deafening. She glanced up when he dragged a chair over to where she was sitting, positioning it so that she had absolutely no choice but to be aware of his proximity.

'I'm sorry I haven't prepared any salad for you,' she said politely. 'You made it clear that you weren't going to be around.'

'I don't like salad. I prefer to leave that stuff to the rabbits to dispose of. I needed to talk to you.'

'Good. Because, actually, *I* need to talk to *you*.' Maude pushed the plate to one side, sat back and folded her arms. 'I've come to the conclusion that this trip might have been a good idea at the start, but it's been a number of days, and I feel it's time for me to return to London. If you don't mind, I will take a few days off work, perhaps as much as a couple of weeks. I'm actually due the time off. I have holiday accrued since...'

'You think I vanished because I didn't want to spend time in your company?'

'Don't be nuts. Why would I think that?' But she went beetroot-red. 'I know this is a working holiday for you! And I hope you haven't come in here because you...because you feel guilty at leaving me to my own devices.'

'You were hurt. I could see it on your face.'

'I was *not*.' Maude wondered whether this conversation could get any worse.

'I had to leave because I wasn't sure whether I was going to end up making a nuisance of myself.'

'I have no idea what you're talking about.'

'When I came back here earlier and saw you in the pool, Maude...' He raked his fingers through his hair and sat back, briefly closing his eyes. 'I don't think you have the slightest idea how you look.'

'How I *look*?' Maude was prepared to be indignant but something about those dark eyes fastened on her was bringing her out in a cold sweat.

She found that she was fidgeting with the wine glass and sorted that problem by gulping down the lot and pushing the glass to one side.

'Sexy,' Mateo muttered huskily. 'That swimsuit... your body...'

'Me?'

'You. Don't look so shocked. You must have known that I am attracted to you, Maude? You must have felt it when we kissed at the party and then later…?'

'You *can't* be attracted to me! Not really.'

'What does that mean? I'm sitting here and it's all I can do not to reach out and touch you.'

'You're *you*, Mateo,' Maude said helplessly as she grappled to keep a hold on common sense.

'What is that supposed to mean?'

'You could have anyone you want. I *know* the sort of women you want. I know the sort of women men go for and it's not strapping brunettes with careers!'

'Maude, you've lost me. What the hell are you talking about?'

'I lost my heart to someone once!' she burst out impulsively. 'It was when I first went to university. His name was Colin and he was just about everything I knew wouldn't look at me twice…he was tall, dark and handsome and smart…but he *did* look at me and we went out for a few months before…'

She felt her eyes sting and was cross with herself because that was all a lifetime ago, and afterwards, she'd known that she hadn't been in love with the guy at all. She'd just had a coming-of-age moment, destined to be lost in the mists of time.

'Before…?' Mateo prompted gravely. He leant towards her, reached for her hand and she didn't pull away.

'Before he found true love with a petite blonde.'

'What happened years ago has nothing to do with what's happening right here, right now. Nothing to do with what my body feels whenever you're around. I'm not comfortable telling you this, because I don't like not being able to control my own responses, but it seems like in this instance my body has other ideas. I couldn't stay away today like I'd planned, and I couldn't work for the rest of the evening knowing you were around, also like I'd planned.'

Maude looked away, face burning, and her body aflame at what he was saying.

'Look at me, Maude.' He gently tilted her chin so that she was staring at him, wide-eyed and in a state of shock. 'I'm attracted to you, it's as simple as that. I don't know what to do with this attraction but I felt I had to get it out in the open.'

He paused and tilted his head to one side, his eyes searching hers. 'You had a crap experience with a guy you met when you were younger and you've let that play into a narrative about the way you look. For reasons that baffle me, you somehow never gained self-confidence when it came to appearances, so you relied on your brains instead to see you through. I'm guessing you don't want to be hurt by anyone again. Am I right?'

'No one mentioned anything about that,' Maude muttered.

'That's as may be but…' He hesitated. 'This thing I feel…this isn't about love, Maude.' He smiled crookedly. 'Despite the fact that we're supposed to be a pair of love birds on course to a lifetime of happy-ever-afters. This is about attraction. It's about my eyes following you and my hands longing to touch. It's about having to take cold showers because when I think of you my body goes into overdrive. The world may think one thing but we know different. We've found ourselves in a peculiar situation but this isn't about love, is it?'

'No. No, it's not. Of course it's not!'

'People get hurt because they hand their emotions over to someone else's caretaking. That's not what this is about. For me? This is about a pull I can't shake. I want to sleep with you, and I'm telling you this because if you're not of the same mind set then tell me. Tell me and you have my word that this conversation ends here.'

'I…'

'Are you attracted to me, Maude?'

Maude squirmed. She was a grown woman and yet she felt like a teenager dealing with feelings and emotions for the first time. But, truthfully, this *was* a first, wasn't it? All her life she had linked sex with love. After Colin, she had made up her mind that she would never compromise when it came to guys. She had her checklist and she had ticked off their suitability as long-term partners—even the handful of guys she had dated casually had been ticked off. They'd been found wanting before bed had ever reared its head.

But Mateo…

He was so unsuitable, sitting there, luring her into

something that promised nothing…just a couple of ships passing in the night…

Her body tingled at the thought of him touching it and she breathed in deeply, shakily.

Was this what she had been missing in her life? Had she wasted too much time searching for Mr Right, when Mr Utterly Wrong might be just the tonic she needed?

Had she spent way too long living in her comfort zone, too timid to venture out?

Heart beating like a sledgehammer, Maude lowered her eyes and then said, 'Yes. Yes, I am, Mateo Moreno. I'm attracted to you…'

CHAPTER SIX

'So what do you think we should do about this?' Mateo murmured huskily.

Sweet anticipation filled him but there was no way he was going to rush anything. Instinct told him that she wasn't tough like the women he was accustomed to dating. She said she was attracted to him and, leaning into him as she was, her eyes bright with tentative sincerity, there was not a bit of him that doubted her.

But he wanted her to feel secure enough with him to follow through with what she'd said. Whether he spontaneously combusted out of sheer frustration didn't matter.

'There's no one here at the moment, aside from us...'

Mateo relaxed. His smile was slow and wicked. 'Deep down,' he murmured, 'Maybe you decided to be prepared to seduce me when I got back... Get rid of the staff, and you would be free to pounce on an innocent guy...'

Maude burst out laughing. Moving closer seemed the most natural thing in the world to do because here they were and, against all odds, he made her feel utterly relaxed and comfortable with his light teasing.

She'd just made a monumental, earth shattering decision to *live in the moment* and, if she'd thought that she might be riven with self-doubt, then she was proved wrong as he stood, pulling her towards him as he did so, and then cupped her buttocks with his hands and shifted her so that she felt the stiffness of his erection.

Maude's legs turned to jelly. Her hands were flat on his chest and she worked them slowly and cautiously over his shoulders, and sighed at the packed muscle under her fingers.

His mouth when it touched hers was soft and gentle and she relaxed into a slow, lingering kiss, the kiss of someone with all the time in the world and in no hurry.

The yearning for more built as they continued to kiss. His tongue meshed with hers in a lazy exploration of her mouth and her hands crept from his shoulders to his neck, caressing and feeling the warmth of his skin with something akin to wonder.

His hair was springy when she sifted her fingers through it, just as he brought his hands up to curve her waist and then to rest lightly on her breasts.

'Upstairs…please…' She struggled to gasp the words out and Mateo drew back and smiled.

'Your wish is my command but…are you sure about this, Maude?'

'I'm sure.'

She met his eyes steadily. Whatever the carousel that could be called his love life, and however much she had always disapproved of men who veered from one woman to another like a spoiled toddler given free run in a candy shop, she couldn't help but be impressed by his genuine concern for her.

She knew that, if she were to slap him down now, he would do just as he had said. He would walk away and he would never, ever mention it again.

She held his hand and tugged him behind her towards the kitchen door.

'I've always loved a woman who takes the lead,' he said. 'It fulfils my craving to be dominated.'

Maude laughed again over her shoulder. 'You should be careful what you wish for,' said this reckless, daring young woman she barely recognised as herself.

'Why? Are you promising me some kinky stuff between the sheets?'

Maude paused, suddenly worried, and she moved to gaze at him with serious eyes,

'I should warn you, Mateo…'

'Shh.' Mateo placed a finger over her lips and smiled. 'Don't say a word. We're going to have fun and that's it. If you want to tie me to the bed posts and have your wicked way, then I'm more than willing to give it a go, but there'll be no pressure on you to do anything at all you don't feel comfortable doing.'

'How do you do that?' Maude whispered.

'What?'

'Make me feel so at ease.'

'There's no need to be nervous. What's happening between us is perfectly natural.'

He led the way this time and she fell into step with him, her hand around his waist, his slung across her shoulders, two people at home with one another, their bodies in sync.

'Haven't you ever been here before?' he asked. 'By which I mean, in a place where you just can't fight the pull of sexual attraction?'

'I...' Maude thought of Colin and struggled to recall his face. She certainly had never felt this way with him. What she'd felt back then had been gentler and a heck of a lot more polite. This...*this*...was like being thrown into the eye of a hurricane, catapulted this way and the other, in the grip of something so powerful all you could do was go along for the ride. 'Not really,' she admitted.

'Not even with the university chap you were in love with?'

'That was ages ago.' Maude marvelled that he had zeroed in on just what had been going through her head. But somehow admitting that this was a first for her, when she knew that it would hardly be a first for *him*, stopped her from telling him the blunt truth. Instead, she laughed and said wryly,

'I'm guessing that being overwhelmed by lust isn't exactly a first for you?'

Why did that hurt?

They were outside his bedroom door.

Mateo paused, hand on the door knob, stilled by her laughing, teasing remark.

Was this just more of the same for him? Mateo had never been a shrinking violet when it came to the opposite sex. He enjoyed women and women enjoyed him. But had he ever been knocked for six like this by any woman? He didn't think so and he frowned because that made no sense.

In passing, he noted that she hadn't expanded on the ex from way back when. Had he been her one big love, leaving a scar that no man had ever been able to smooth over? When Mateo thought about that he felt a stab of something, but he'd never been a jealous guy, so surely that couldn't be it?

This was too much introspection. There was a reason he didn't go down that road. Nothing good ever came from dwelling on things you couldn't change or looking for answers where none were to be found. He'd spent a childhood trying to find out why his mother had walked out on him, and of course there'd been no answers to be found. Since then, he'd accepted the futility of a task like that. He'd learned his lessons and that was the important thing.

'No more talk.' He purred, pushing open the door

and stepping aside for Maude to precede him into the bedroom.

A cool breeze blew through a bank of floor-to-ceiling doors that opened out onto a private black-and-white-tiled patio that housed casual seating. The bedroom was twice the size of hers, and hers was enormous.

She looked around her and he smiled at the direction of her gaze.

'For when I've worked through the night here and couldn't be bothered to use the main offices downstairs.'

She was looking at an impressive desk that sat in its own sectioned space surrounded by a bookcase to the back and a bank of hand-made teak cabinets to one side.

'Do you ever stop working?'

Mateo shot her a slashing, sexy smile that turned her legs to jelly and he strolled towards her.

'You're about to find out.' He played with the lobe of her ear, eliciting a sigh of capitulation, before tracing the outline of her mouth with his finger, then his tongue, before picking up kissing where they had left off.

Maude wound her arms around his neck. She was a tall, well-built woman and yet, mysteriously, he made her feel ultra-feminine and protected. His arms were bands of steel. When her hands slid to feel him, softly exploring over his shirt, she felt hard muscle and sinew.

The heat and damp between her legs made her squirm. Maude, who had spent so long single-mindedly pursuing her career, was an innocent when it came to the opposite sex. She'd genuinely had no idea that she could be so overtaken by desire that she could barely keep a thought in her head.

He tilted back her head and trailed hot kisses along her neck, one hand coiled into her hair, the other sliding along her side, dipping into her waist and skimming over her thigh.

They staggered to the king-sized bed and Maude fell back on the softest of silken covers, immediately propping herself up to watch as Mateo reached for a remote, pressed a button and activated the smooth glide of shutters across the open windows, blocking out the light and plunging the room into cosy semi-darkness.

He didn't head for the bed—not yet. Instead, he stood, his back to the windows, hand on the zipper of his trousers resting there and teasing her so that she wanted to yell at him to *hurry up*.

He took his time undressing, and Maude didn't want to blink because she didn't want to miss a thing.

The shirt came off and he flung it to the ground, then the trousers, and when he stepped out of them only the boxers were left, through which she could detect the bulge of his erection.

He adjusted himself, cupping his erection and then leaving his hand on it before ridding himself of the last barrier to total nakedness.

Maude drew in a sharp breath.

Mateo Moreno, the guy she had surreptitiously looked at for so many months safe in the knowledge that he would never glance twice in her direction, was now standing in front of her completely naked.

And what a magnificent sight he made.

'Like what you see?' He half-smiled as he walked towards the bed to stand right next to her. 'Feel free to touch me wherever you like...'

Maude moaned softly, fell back against the pillows and shut her eyes as she heard him laugh under his breath.

'Everything about you turns me on,' he said, sinking onto the mattress alongside her. He positioned her so that they were facing one another. She still had all her clothes on. How did that make sense?

But instinct told her that he wasn't going to rush. She was here because she wanted to be here—she had told him that, had practically led him up to the bedroom and was now going crazy with wanting him—but still...

He would give her all the time in the world because he wanted this to be just right, wanted her to feel safe, and she really did feel safe.

Moreover, she didn't feel self-conscious. How had he made that possible?

'Like what?' she asked, and he grinned and kissed the tip of her nose.

'You're smart, you're funny and you're sexy as hell. What's not to like?'

'I'm new,' she challenged with a smile. 'I'm a novelty.'

'And maybe that's what I am as well,' he suggested.

'Maybe you are.'

'Which brings me to the fact that, once again, we're talking too much.'

'Is that something you're not into doing when you're in bed with a woman?'

'As a general rule, I tend to leave the chit chat at the bedroom door.' He slipped his hand under her top and rested it on her stomach, feeling her quiver. 'One more thing to add to the list of things about you that turn me on—I like the way you respond to me.'

'That's very egotistic,' Maude said lazily, her breath catching in her throat when he cupped her breast and began massaging it.

'I'll take that as a compliment. Now, enough! I want to go slow but, hell, I want to see you delectable and naked on my sheets a whole lot more.'

He stripped her of her clothing.

Bit by slow bit, she was shorn of her top, her trousers, until he was gazing down at her and she was in just her undies and her bra.

He was straddling her and he was turned on, his erection bold and throbbing. She sensed that he was hanging on by a thread and she felt a heady power that this beautiful, sexy guy could be so hot for her.

He groaned, cupped her breasts and said something thick in Italian that she didn't understand, but didn't need to, because his expression was saying everything she wanted to hear.

She was every single thing he'd never known he needed. That was going through Mateo's head as he toyed with her nipples, large, circular discs that were testing his resolve to the max. He desperately wanted this to last, wanted to take his time, but he knew he wasn't going to.

He sank into her breasts, teased the bulbous nipples with his tongue, nipped them gently with his teeth and felt soaring satisfaction at the mewls of pleasure that came from her as she tossed underneath him, her eyes shut, her mouth parted, her breathing fast and shallow.

He reached behind and groped to feel her underwear then pushed his hand underneath until he found the slick, wet groove between her legs.

He worked his magic in two different places, sending her into another world.

'Please stop or I won't be able to…to…'

'To come against my finger?' Mateo asked huskily and she nodded, face burning as she sped towards the point of no return. Their eyes tangled and he kissed her, a thorough, heated kiss while he continued doing what he was doing, bringing her to the peak of satisfaction until she spasmed in an orgasm that took her away.

Mateo let her cool down. He was so turned on, it was a physical ache. He forced himself to go slow, built himself up bit by bit in stages, stilling her hand when she wanted to touch him because he knew that, if she did, he would go the way she just had, and he wanted to be deep inside her for his release.

Maude's body was so in tune with his. *She* felt so in tune with *him*. She didn't understand how that was possible. She didn't get how he could make her feel so comfortable, so uninhibited, when everything inside her said it should be just the opposite.

She stroked him, she let him take his time, murmuring into his ear; and, when he reached for protection from the bedside drawer, she was blossoming once again inside, yearning for him, her body tingling all over.

He took her to heights she'd never imagined possible. Her fingers dug into his back as she writhed under him and, when he came, arching up and straining with the force of his orgasm, she followed shortly after.

Spent, she flipped onto her back and stared up at the ceiling.

'Regrets?'

She turned when he asked this to find him looking at her with brooding intensity.

'No.'

'Sure?'

'I'm not a kid, Mateo. I'm good at following through when I've made my mind up about something.'

'I know.' He smiled. 'Just for the record, no regrets from me either.'

'I guess I should head back to my room—or we could go downstairs and have something to eat. It's still quite early.'

'I'm relieved you didn't suggest doing some work.'

'Am I that boring?' Her voice was light but there was hurt underlying it. He wasn't to know that *work* was the wall she had built around herself to protect her from the slings and arrows of doubt and uncertainty. It always had been.

'Anything but.' He smiled and tucked her hair behind her ear, then left his hand there to cup her cheek. 'You can try as hard as you like to duck behind that professional mask you enjoy wearing, but I've seen behind that mask now and the woman there is the least boring woman I've ever known.'

Maude reddened.

'I don't duck behind anything...' she protested, but feebly, and his eyebrows shot up.

'Don't you? I think, whenever you're confronted with anything you find a little too much out of your comfort zone, you revert to work because that's your safe place. I'm not sure you even realise it, Maude. Perhaps it's a habit that's become so ingrained that it's part of you, but maybe it's stopped you from the business of going with the flow and seeing what happens next.'

'There's such a thing as doing too much of that *going with the flow* stuff,' Maude muttered uncomfortably, because he had hit the nail on the head, and he burst out laughing.

'My darling, you're so very right.'

Which for some reason made her feel very good inside. He added casually, 'Now that we're engaged…and these are my personal thoughts, to be shot down in flames if you so wish… I think we should carry on with what we have here.'

But for how long…?

This was what Maude thought as she lounged back in her chair, Mateo next to her, both sipping iced coffee and people-watching, backs to the bustling chi-chi café as they looked at the people coming and going.

Both were behind dark sunglasses.

Undoubtedly, he looked considerably more sophisticated than her, his skin burnished bronzed from the time spent under Tuscan skies. She noticed how people, both men and women, slid sideways glances at him when they walked past, as though wondering whether he was famous, whether they should recognise him behind those dark sunglasses.

'This is the longest I've ever been out of an office for a while,' he had confessed only the night before, lying in bed after a session of passionate sex.

They had only been in Tuscany for ten days, and it beggared belief how little time he seemed to spend relaxing.

But he was relaxing now. So was she—bliss. She was enjoying the heat of the sun and the pleasure of being in Siena, sitting in a mediaeval square surrounded by buildings that looked as though they had been there since time immemorial, all of them weathered and the colour of faded, water-coloured sepia, each so exquisitely fashioned that it was a feast for the eye.

They had spent the day shopping. It was the first time she had ever shopped with a guy and she had loved the way he'd made her feel when she'd paraded outfits for him.

He'd made her feel special.

He made her feel special now, their fingers loosely entwined on the wrought-iron table between them, an intimate gesture that warmed her.

But for how long? For how much longer could this continue...?

Reality awaited them. As predicted, they had been a flash in the pan when it had come to the tabloids, soon overtaken by celebrities doing stupid things or getting into trouble.

And what about his ex? From even further away in LA, where she was apparently back on the catwalk and doing the social scene, she had sent a text telling him that she'd met someone and sarcastically wishing him the best with his new woman.

Maude had done her bit and, if Cassie was poised in the wings, waiting for the fallout of her mischief-making to rain down, then this charade had served its purpose because Cassie had apparently given up the ghost when it came to trying to climb back into a relationship with Mateo. She would have the last laugh when the engagement she had engineered came to its predictable end. She'd think he would be massively inconvenienced and she would be rather pleased with herself.

And her family... Maude had sent a couple of sneaky selfies to them, but her mother was busy with the finishing touches to the wedding and just content that her daughter was doing a bit more than working eight to eight in an office, ignoring her pleas to find herself a good man.

She'd found the good man and all was right in the world. Except, it wasn't, was it?

'Penny for them.'

Maude felt Mateo's eyes resting on her and she sighed. 'I'm thinking how wonderful all of this is,' she said truthfully.

'Don't tell me you've never been to Italy before?' he said gently. 'Isn't this the playground for the English middle classes?'

'You're very cynical, Mateo Moreno.'

'Old habits die hard. But am I right?'

'I've been before,' she confessed. 'But not for a long time and never like this.'

'Like this?'

With someone I'm falling for...

'Not...being shuffled here and there by parents who want to cram in as much as they can with two pre-adolescent kids.'

Her heart was beating fast and she felt a slick of perspiration form a film over her.

Was that what was happening—was this a slow path towards falling in love with this guy? Yes. How and when, she didn't know. She just knew that this was where she'd ended up—on track to losing her heart to a heart breaker, to becoming another notch on the bedpost. Because, however much of a gentleman Mateo could be, he was still the inveterate bachelor who had no intention of settling down.

She'd disobeyed every rule she had ever taken care to lay down for herself and had drifted into love—and what a hopeless love it was.

He was smiling, his voice a lazy drawl as he sympathised with a twelve-year-old Maude wanting to wriggle out of traipsing around churches and looking at boring old statues.

She wasn't even listening. Appalled, her mind was throwing up a series of scenarios, each worse than the one before. How desperate he had been to get rid of his clingy ex—would he be equally desperate to get rid of *her* should he find out what she felt for him? She pictured him fleeing into the dead of night and then disappearing without a trace.

'My mum wants me to head back home,' Maude said abruptly. She turned to look at him and faked a smile, relieved that she could hide behind her sunglasses. 'Something to do with flowers and bridesmaids.' She smiled ruefully. 'And I guess it's time we left this paradise behind. It's safe to say that the hounds have found other trails to sniff. We're old news.'

'Flowers and bridesmaids?'

'Happens when there's a wedding and your mum is a perfectionist,' Maude hedged vaguely.

'When did you have in mind?'

'Perhaps in the morning?' She smiled again but inside her heart was breaking in two. 'Or is that too soon for…er…things to be put in place?'

'That could work.'

Mateo tried not to scowl. How easy to destroy a good moment! Of course she was right, he grudgingly admitted—he was a workaholic, wasn't he? And there was work waiting for him in London—lots of it.

So, why exactly was he here, basking in the sun, watching the world go by?

Because of the woman indolently lounging next to him. She'd bewitched him. Little by little, she'd cast a net around him, seducing him into a holiday frame of mind which had made him lazy and…*content*.

Unease slithered through him because this sort of situation was not one he had ever courted, or ever wanted to. As much as she pulled him to her, weaving spells he couldn't resist, so instinct pushed him back, obeying laws of survival embedded inside him.

It was almost as though she had taken sandpaper to him and softened his edges, but Mateo knew that he needed those edges. Without them, life risked losing structure and that wasn't going to happen.

So, did they return to London?

Definitely.

If he wasn't as relieved as he should have been with her suggestion, if there was a scrap of him that hankered for a bit more of this truant-playing, then it was simply because she had beat him to saying what had to be said. He was usually the one who took the lead in this sort of situation.

'And once we're back,' she suggested thoughtfully, 'I'm thinking I could take a fortnight off and head back up home to help.'

'Isn't your mother in control of everything, except whatever's going on with flowers and bridesmaids?'

'She would never actually *ask* for help,' Maude said, sticking to the truth as much as she could. 'Which doesn't mean she wouldn't *welcome* it.'

She gave his hand a quick squeeze and looked away, detaching her fingers to twine them together while she waited for him to respond, to take the conversation to its natural conclusion, which would surely be a discussion about *them*.

She flirted with the forbidden hope that, faced with this cautious ultimatum, he might declare undying love for her, tell her that he couldn't bear the thought of them returning. That hope lasted a matter of seconds, while into the silence she read something else, something that made her blood run cold.

What if he asked her just to prolong this? They made great love together. She knew that he enjoyed her as much as she enjoyed him, and she also knew that he was not a guy who was into self-denial. From his point of view, she was on the same page as he was. A charade started in good faith had turned into something else, and now here they were, so why not just 'go with the flow' as he was fond of encouraging her? It would fizzle out in due course, but they would have non-committal fun in the meantime.

Maude could think of nothing worse. The only way she could think to deal with this, to deal with her silly heart which she'd handed over to him on a platter, was to cut herself free. Rip off the plaster, suck up the pain and wait for it to pass.

At the end of a fortnight away from him, she would be in a better place, more able to distance herself. She could request a transfer. She could quit her job and find something else. There were options.

One of those options wasn't waiting for him to suggest something she knew she would be sorely tempted to take.

Before he could say anything, she plunged in.

'Let's enjoy what we have here, Mateo. It's been... time out for us. Weird but invigorating...and no regrets.'

'Explain.'

Around them people came and went, and it felt odd to have this jarring conversation surrounded by such beauty.

'When we return to London...tomorrow...then I think we should end this. It's not as though either of us is in it for anything more than a bit of fun, is it?'

Mateo turned to face her and she likewise looked at him. Now he lifted the sunglasses to his forehead and lifted off hers, so that their eyes tangled, so that he could see what was going through her head. But there was nothing there to see, no thoughts revealed.

He dangled her sunglasses on one finger and with a frown gazed directly into her blue eyes.

'Is this the sound of you dumping me?' he asked softly, with teasing amusement even though he was, frankly, incredulous.

'It's the sound of me doing what needs to be done,' Maude returned. 'Wouldn't you agree?'

No, Mateo thought. It was the sound of her hurting him, because there was a pain inside him, an ache at the thought of never touching her again, never being able to reach for her in the night.

There had been times in the early hours of the morning, still half-asleep in the stillness of the dark, when he had wondered whether he had dreamt some of the sex they'd had.

Sex with no protection.

Once. Twice. The mere fact that he was only thinking about this now was worrying enough in itself. Never mind the even more worrying notion that he had somehow become stupidly addicted to her nearness, to the sound of her laughter, to the way she enjoyed arguing with him, to her fierce intelligence mixed with that peculiar vulnerability that she was always at such pains to hide. There was a chill inside him, something dangerous and unpredictable stirring, something to be fought against.

Shutters dropped.

'Absolutely,' he drawled, pushing the sunglasses back in place and dropping hers on the table.

He signalled for the bill without taking his eyes off her. 'Tell me what happens next. I like a woman who takes charge. And you're right—absolutely the correct thing to do. Business and pleasure? Never makes for a good mix.'

'Agreed.' Her smile looked frozen. 'I'm glad you're not…not…upset.'

'*Upset?*' Mateo laughed shortly. 'I think you must be confusing me with someone else. So what's the way forward? We head back…you take your time out with flowers and bridesmaids and then the wedding…?'

'Which, I think you'll agree, it's probably wise for you to skip. Now that we've decided on a way forward, there's no point feeding the illusion that this is some kind of love match. Which it isn't.' Maude paused just for a few seconds. She could feel the heat burning her cheeks.

'Don't you think your parents might be a bit alarmed that your fiancé isn't around on such an important occasion?'

'They'd be more alarmed if you didn't show up at *our* important occasion.' The joke fell flat. 'I've sent them a couple of photos of here and of you, and before we head back today I can get someone to take some shots of us. I'll just tell them that you were called away on business and after that—'

'Bridges to be crossed,' Mateo interjected levelly. He gave her a mock salute but there was no humour in his smile. 'Well, my darling, here's to a short-lived but highly enjoyable engagement. Tomorrow is another day…'

CHAPTER SEVEN

MAUDE STOOD IN front of the wine bar where she had
arranged to meet Mateo.

She could have chosen the office. She could have
chosen his house in Chelsea. But she had ditched
both options—the office because she wasn't sure
she could bear the curious looks of the people she
had worked with, and his house because that reeked
of the desperation of an ex who refused to leave him
alone. Besides, she hadn't relished the thought of seeing him in his natural habitat, surrounded by stuff
that might weaken her defences.

So here she was. Standing in front of a trendy pub
in Kensington, one half of which was gastro, with
fashionable rustic tables and cool, colourful mis-
matched chairs, and the other half pub, with a semi-
circular bar and lots of stools by a high counter and
squat, square tables and chairs.

It had been nearly three weeks since she had last
seen him. They had spent that last night together.
They had made love and she had smiled through it

all, knowing that she was saying goodbye to a place to which she would never return but one that would leave lasting damage to her heart.

It had been intense. Maude had wanted to take everything she could from that last time she got to feel his nakedness, got to enjoy the way he touched her, the way he responded to her touching him. She wanted to fill herself up to the brim *with him* and commit every single detail to memory.

They had parted on excellent terms. She had kept that smile on her face and he had been perfectly happy with the end of their affair. She suspected that he'd been thoroughly relieved that she had done the dirty work and called the whole thing off, without putting him in the awkward position of having to give her the brush-off.

She'd then headed to Berkshire. She could have popped up there now and again to help out, but she chose to stay instead, because she knew that keeping herself busy would clear her head.

'But honestly, darling, what about your work?' her mother had questioned, for once concerned about the career she had previously despaired of.

'Holiday,' Maude had responded. 'Also, Mateo is…er…away, I'm afraid, for most of the coming month with huge deal in the Far East… Globetrotting…always on the move… Not ideal, to be honest!'

And so his non-appearance at the wedding had been glossed over. And in fairness it had been such a busy time that in-depth questioning had been avoided.

But foundations had been put in place. Amy had casually asked her about an engagement ring. 'Not,' she had hastily added, 'That anyone really cares about that kind of thing any more...'

Maude had looked saddened and had made noises about whether she was doing the right thing with Mateo.

'I want a guy who's going to be around for me,' she had said vaguely but sincerely, which had been nothing but the truth. 'Not a guy who's married to his work. What starts out in good faith can end up crashing and burning in the face of reality.'

Amy had been far too busy to probe but Maude had planted seeds, and what else could she have done? But, in her head and in her aching heart, Mateo refused to be consigned to the past.

The wedding day had been hard as she had watched the joyful couple, the love they shared, cruel reminders of what she so desperately wanted in the end with Mateo—the happy-ever-after future Amy and her brother were united in finding, and what she knew she would never have, because she had foolishly fallen for a guy who was incapable of giving it.

As soon as the wedding was out of the way, she had headed back to London, emailed Human Resources and quit her job.

Tellingly, Mateo had had nothing to say about that.

Had he spared her a second's thought?

He had texted her on the day of the wedding to tell

her that he hoped it had all gone well and had sent the couple a ridiculously expensive set of high-end luggage as a present, apologising for his absence.

In return, she had texted him back, informing him that she was going to hand in her notice, that it was for the best and that she knew he would be pleased to hear that she was making great headway in finding an out for their so-called relationship. She had ended the text with a friendly winking emoji, keeping it light-hearted.

Things would all work out in the end, she had told herself. Broken hearts mended. Time was a great healer.

She had been badly prepared for the unexpected.

She had not really paid attention to the fact that her period had failed to show up when it should have, even though she was as regular as clockwork.

She had not even really braced herself for that little stick giving her a positive result when she had reluctantly decided to buy the pregnancy testing kit.

It had all come as a shock.

Instead of spending the first week on her return to London looking for a new job, she had spent it in a daze doing three more tests, staring at each positive result with the same shock every single time.

Until she had finally done what she knew she needed to do. She had texted Mateo and requested a meeting.

Right here—in a public place, busy but not too busy, quiet but not too quiet.

She propelled herself forward. The sunny skies they had left behind weeks ago were no longer in evidence. Instead, it was a grey day with a light drizzle dampening everything, still warm, but not warm enough for any of the sundresses she had shoved in a trunk and stuffed into a cupboard because they reminded her of Tuscany.

She was wearing a pair of trousers, trainers, a short-sleeved tee-shirt and an anorak. Not exactly chic, but that was the last thing on Maude's mind as she took a deep breath and headed inside to meet Mateo.

Mateo had no idea how keyed up he was about this out of the blue meeting until he saw her.

Three weeks. With a push, and much to his fury, he could practically count the time in minutes and seconds. He hated it because it smacked of emotional weakness which was something he had no time for.

She'd dumped him. That was the long and short of it. The guy who was never dumped had been dumped.

She'd walked out on him and hadn't looked back, and Mateo had not been able to get her out of his mind ever since she'd done that.

Why?

Was it because he was so damned arrogant that his pride had been wounded? He liked to think himself bigger than that, but then the only alternative was one he had no intention of accepting—she was still in his head because he missed her. He'd grown accustomed to her being around. He no longer enjoyed the solitude of an empty bed. She'd opened his eyes to the joy of spending the night with someone sleeping next to him, and then she'd vanished and taken that joy away with her...

Mateo had buried himself in work and taken himself out of the country, returning to bury himself in work once again, but for the first time in his life it had failed to do the trick.

And then she'd texted him to meet up.

She'd had time to think, had time to work out just how good what they'd shared had been—that was the obvious and only conclusion he could read into her desire to meet him. Because he knew that everything had progressed and finalised when it came to her handing in her notice. He hadn't stood in the way, hadn't demanded she work out her notice, but indeed had given her a glowing reference. He expected some people might think he'd been biased, because they'd been an item, but Mateo could not care less because he'd never allowed other people's opinions to influence his behaviour.

So, she obviously wanted to pick up where they'd left off, at which point Mateo was torn.

He wanted her back.

They'd had a good thing going and it was only natural to want to prolong it. Why not? And, on the plus side, wasn't it always better to let things reach their natural conclusion? If he didn't, wasn't there the danger of experiencing the frustration of an incomplete situation? A painful, driving need to see things through?

But Mateo knew that this was not a normal situation. In truth, his preoccupation with Maude had made him uneasy and wary. It would be important to lay down ground rules just in case they had become blurred in the interim. He wasn't into longevity with any woman and nothing had changed.

All these things had gone through his head when he had read her brief text. A 'when and where' text, brisk and to the point, which he had appreciated. No need to state urgency when it was a given.

For the first time in weeks, he had felt…*content*.

Now, as he watched her glance around, frowning as she tried to locate him, anticipation rippled through him.

God, he'd missed her body—her generous curves, the feel of her breasts weighing heavily in his big hands…

All of her… He'd missed the whole package deal.

She was dressed in the sort of frightful outfit that had become a thing of the past when they'd been in Italy but, for some weird reason, he found he didn't mind. The fewer stares she got, the better, as far as he was concerned. He almost laughed at that sudden bout of old-fashioned possessiveness.

Since when had he morphed into a chauvinist? Not him at all!

He signalled to her and saw a shadow of hesitation cross her face before she headed to where he was sitting at one of the low tables in the bar area.

He'd ordered a bottle of wine in advance of their meeting, an excellent red. Not one from his vineyard, of course, but from the region. He'd be interested in hearing what she thought of it. For someone who wasn't particularly interested in drinking wine, she had a pretty good palate, as he had discovered in Tuscany.

'Maude…' Mateo rose to greet her. He reminded himself that, however satisfying it was to know that they were once again on the same page, he would still have to lay down his boundary lines. He might feel oddly out of control when it came to her, but laying down those lines would be a reminder to himself. He was still a guy in charge.

'Hi.'

Now that she was here, standing in front of Mateo, overwhelmed by him once again, she was wondering whether she'd done the right thing in coming.

'Don't look so apprehensive. Shall we retreat to the dining area? Are you hungry?'

'It's fine here. I… I won't be here long.'

Mateo frowned. 'There's no rush.' He delivered one of those killer smiles that always made her weak at the knees and which made her go weak at the knees now. 'I've cleared my calendar for you.' He waited until she was sitting, until wine had been poured for both of them and the hovering waiter had left, with an order for some tapas, before he continued, the killer smile abruptly dropping to be replaced by an expression of deadly seriousness.

'Look, I know that you're finding this awkward.'

'You do?'

'Yes. It's written all over your face. Don't forget, I know you as well as I know the back of my hand. At least it seems that way to me. You're finding this awkward, and I don't blame you, but I'm glad you're here. Glad that you've come back to me.'

'Come back to you...'

'I've been thinking about you as well. I'd go so far as to say that I've been missing...our passionate nights together. And days.' The smile returned and his eyes darkened. 'I've discovered that an empty bed is way too big when the woman I should be sharing it with is no longer in it. Which is why I don't want you to feel awkward. We're in the same place, Maude, we want the same thing. And I think we can both be honest and admit that giving one another up was good in theory but crap in practice.'

'Hmm.'

'But...' Mateo let that single word hover in the air between them, inviting her to look at him with questioning blue eyes.

'But?' Maude politely parroted.

'*But*...this is the first time I've ever done anything like this.'

'Anything like what?'

'For me,' Mateo elaborated, 'When a relation-ship ends, it ends. There's no going back.' He smiled wryly. 'I would say even more so in the case of a re-lationship that ends because a woman has been the one to do the walking. Not that I would know that for sure, because it's never happened before.'

'I'm sure,' Maude said, even more politely.

'But because this is a first for me…well, how do I put this?… I don't want you to read anything into it.'

'Read anything?'

'What we had was pure and simple. We had great sex. I'm very happy to pick up where we left off.'

'Ah. I understand. You want to make sure I know that this is just a meaningless affair that has a time-line.'

Mateo frowned and shifted.

He had finished his glass and poured himself an-other, but realised that she had failed to take a single sip of hers, sticking to water instead. The tapas had been delivered to them. He had barely noticed the arrival of the waiter. He'd been utterly wrapped up in the glow of anticipation and the urgency of mak-ing sure he told it like it was, no room for misun-derstandings.

Now, he realised that she had contributed remark-ably little to the conversation and she certainly hadn't shown any of the enthusiasm he had expected.

Why? It wasn't as though he had tried to dissuade her, was it? The contrary! He had been open and honest about wanting her back in his life as much as she clearly wanted him back in hers.

'That's not how I would have phrased it,' he said stiffly.

Maude shrugged.

'I'm not here to get back together with you, Mateo,' she clarified.

'What? Come again?'

Their eyes tangled and Maude could see his puzzlement. Why else would she possibly have arranged this meeting if not to coerce herself back into his life?

Yet she could see why he thought as he did. There had been no need for her to sit through the past forty minutes of him telling her that he wanted her back, and she was ashamed that she felt something warm and satisfying inside at the thought that he still wanted her, still desired her. Nothing to do with love, of course, because that was not what they had ever been about. He had stated that boldly and clearly.

Yet how wonderful it felt to be wanted by him… To have those husky words wash over her, reminding her of how they had made one another feel, how he had made *her* feel—alive for the first time in her life, a woman encouraged to enjoy her sexual appetites with a man who couldn't get enough of them.

Surely she was only human in greedily wanting to take those titbits and hold onto them for a bit?

'Mateo, I'm pregnant,' she said flatly and watched as the colour drained from his face.

'Sorry, I don't think I quite caught that.'

'I'm having a baby. That's why I arranged to see you.'

'But…*no*. That isn't possible. It can't be. *No*. Impossible!'

He flung himself back and raked his fingers through his hair, and for a few seconds he looked away from her and stared blindly over to the bar. Maude read that as the reaction of a guy desperately trying to find a way out of a nightmare he hadn't invited.

She felt for him. She knew that this was the last thing in the world he would have expected to hear and, even as those words had left her lips, she knew that they would shatter the world as he had knew it.

But not for a single second had she considered *not* saying anything to him. That would have been utterly unfair. How he dealt with the news would be up to him, but she had to let him know, in a hurry, that she hadn't dropped this bombshell to mess up his life.

'How could that have happened? How? I was careful…'

'There were a couple of times,' Maude murmured, 'When being careful wasn't top of the agenda. In the early hours of the morning. I didn't make a note of dates and times but I'm sure you can remember…'

'It felt like a dream, that one time…twice…' Mateo muttered. 'This can't be happening.'

'I came here because it was the right thing to do, not because I want anything from you.'

'I'm not following you.' Mateo frowned. Everything felt disjointed. He looked at her. What he saw was a woman with his baby inside her, and it was tearing him apart, because a child had never been in his game plan. But *his* child! He could barely follow what she was saying.

'I won't need rescuing,' Maude said gently. 'I know this has probably blown your world apart, but don't think that you owe me anything. Neither of us is to blame. In the heat of the moment, things happen, and sometimes those things have consequences that are unexpected.'

'I can't believe this is happening. When did you find out?'

'A week ago.'

'You've known about this for *a week*? And it took you that long to make your way here?'

The incredulous condemnation in his voice made her hackles rise and she narrowed her eyes.

'I was adjusting to the situation myself,' she said coolly. 'Your world's been tilted on its axis but so has mine. You're not the only one who's been knocked for six, Mateo.'

'No,' he apologised roughly. 'I get that.'

'The point I'm making is that I don't need anything from you. I can manage financially and I can make a loving and rock-solid background for this baby.'

'I really can't believe I'm hearing this.'

'How many times do I have to tell you that mistakes happen?' she said, patience wearing thin, because there were only so many times she could listen to him try and pretend she hadn't said what she had.

'Not that,' Mateo returned with driven urgency. 'What I can't believe is that you actually think that I'm the kind of guy who would walk away from taking responsibility for a child I fathered, with or without planning.' *A baby...a child.* A different world opened up at his feet, and in that world nothing obeyed the laws that had always guided his life choices.

'Well...' Maude went bright red. 'Of course I expect you might want to...take an active part in his or her life...'

'That's very noble-minded of you.' He rallied even though his head was still spinning.

'There's no need to be sarcastic.'

'I think there's every need,' Mateo countered coldly. 'You drop this on me and then, without pausing for breath, you tell me that you don't expect me to do anything with what I've been told. What was your plan ahead, Maude? That I would just conveniently vanish from the scene, letting you do your own thing once your conscience had been cleared?' Shock was still there but fading, giving way to acceptance of a new reality.

'Of course not! I...'

'Have you told your parents?'

'No. Like I said, I've been adjusting to it myself.'

'Good.'

'What do you mean?' Maude was ensnared by the

expression on his face, captivated by all the old attraction she had hoped to navigate her way around after three weeks. It was hopeless. Would she ever be able to get beyond the devastating effect he had on her? Was this what love was all about—exquisite pleasure and then this terrible pain? She felt tears trying to push their way through, and blinked rapidly, because she didn't want to break down.

'Good that you haven't told your parents. We can tell them together.'

'I beg your pardon?'

'We're still engaged, I believe. It shouldn't come as too huge a shock when they find out that we're going to have a baby, or maybe a better way of putting it is that it shouldn't be as much a bolt from the blue.'

'But we're *not* engaged.'

'Let's not lose focus, here, Maude. We're having a baby and I will be at your side when we break the news to them.' He paused. 'And my guess is they will be overjoyed when we tell them that there will be another wedding on the way, and sooner rather than later.'

'What?'

'You came here to tell me that I was allowed to disappear, leaving you to bring our baby up on your own. I'm here to tell you that no such thing is going to happen. The opposite—we're going to be married, Maude.'

He raised his glass and met her gaze with steely

determination. 'A champagne moment but, in the absence of champagne, I'll toast with this excellent wine and you can with sparkling water. A toast to *our* impending big day...'

Maude gaped.

If there were links to what was going on, then she didn't see them.

Hadn't she just been given a speech about his enthusiasm to resume a sex-only relationship with her, no strings attached, because he was a commitment-phobe who wanted nothing more than a bit of fun? How could she now compute that he was sitting here telling her that he wanted to marry her? Since when had 'I'm not into longevity with you' tallied with 'I want us to be married'?

'I'm not following you,' she said slowly. 'You thought I came here to reignite what we had, and you were happy to do that provided I knew that it wasn't going to go anywhere...'

'That was before you told me about the baby.'

'I've already said that I would never get in the way of you seeing him or her. I can manage financially on my own, but likewise, if you want to donate money to the baby's upbringing—'

'Donate? *Donate?*' Mateo exploded with icy fury. 'We're not talking about a local charity here, Maude.'

'Yes, I know that.'

'You're right,' he ground out with wrenching honesty. 'I never thought about a wife or a family but, now that this has been sprung on me, then there's only one solution as far as I am concerned.'

'Which is fine, but it's a situation that involves the two of us, and as far as *I'm* concerned marriage isn't the solution at all, whether or not this has been *sprung* on you.'

'Why not?'

It wasn't just a question, more a challenge contained within a statement, and deep underneath was a barely discernible hint of genuine bewilderment. And it was that bewilderment that softened something inside her and sapped her temptation to argue with him.

'Because we don't love each other,' Maude said huskily. It hurt to say that aloud because it just wasn't true. Her heart was full of love for him.

'But this isn't about us, Maude.'

'It would never work. I look at my parents and they're bonded because they love one another. If they hadn't been, then it would have been a marriage of convenience which would have fizzled out whether kids were involved or not. With the best will in the world, it takes more than a baby to unite two people.'

She looked at him with stubborn determination. 'I'm giving you an out here, Mateo,' she said quietly. 'You can keep the lifestyle you enjoy, go out with whoever you want to go out with, and yet always have however much or little contact with our child as you find comfortable. I really don't understand why you don't find that appealing.'

'You had the luxury of two parents,' he said in a rough undertone. 'You're lucky. Stop to think that there are people like me who never had that luxury. People like me who grew up envious of people like you. I want my child to have what I lacked. I want my child to have the luxury of two parents. When it comes to love, well, it's hit or miss, isn't it? Divorce happens because people get wrapped up in believing in a magic that rarely happens, instead of accepting something that might not be stardust but might just be a lot sturdier. We *like* one another. We *respect* one another. Bring that to the table, and what we would have is a rock-solid union.'

'There would be so much more than that I would expect from a marriage, Mateo.'

Yet what he had said touched her. She had always taken it for granted that marriage was about love, and that without it there could be no such thing. Had she been unrealistic? They were going to have a baby together. For him, above all else, two parents were always going to better than one because he had grown up with just one parent, had lived in the shadow of abandonment. From that had sprung this fierce determination of his to make sure their baby had what he had missed out on.

Two people with two separate dreams.

'What? Tell me.'

'Even if I felt that it was okay to sacrifice my life to a loveless marriage for the sake of a child...'

'Good God, Maude, *sacrifice*...?'

Maude had the grace to flush and when she met his eyes it was to find herself drowning in his incredulous dark gaze.

'Okay, maybe that's a bit—'

'Overblown? Damn right it is.'

'But you know what I mean.'

'Tell me what else you would expect, aside from affection, respect and of course amazing sex. Because let's not beat about the bush here, Maude—we're good in bed together. So tell me what other pieces of the jigsaw have to slot into place before you climb down from a place where only perfection will do.'

His husky reminder of the very thing she had spent the past few weeks trying to shove under the carpet made her go beetroot-red and set up a chain of physical reactions that she couldn't control. Her breasts felt heavy, her nipples pinching against her sensible cotton bra, and there was a shameless pooling of liquid between her legs, an ache there that only served to remind her of just how expert he had been at assuaging it.

And wasn't this why she couldn't end up marrying this guy? The very fact that she loved him made her vulnerable in ways he wouldn't understand.

If she took the love out of marriage, then it would become a business arrangement, and he was right—a business arrangement had a good chance of surviving.

But would *she* be able to survive *it*?

Would she be able to hide her love day after day, week after week and year upon year and content herself with a guy who *liked her* in return?

At what point would those shoots of unhappiness mushroom into full-blown misery and despair? And would that just mean divorce at a later stage when their baby, then a child, would suffer more from the fallout?

The thoughts whirred inside her brain like angry insects and she held her head in her hands for a couple of seconds. When their eyes met, she saw sudden concern in his.

'This is stressing you out.' He raked his fingers through his hair and shook his head. 'That can't be good for you.'

Maude smiled wryly. 'I'll survive, Mateo. It's important we have this discussion. You asked me what other things I would want in any marriage beyond what you've…er…said…'

Mateo tilted his head to one side, his dark eyes still concerned, but thoughtful, his body as still as a statue. His nod was curt.

'Fidelity. Yes, we have great sex at the moment, but that's called lust, and lust doesn't last. What happens when that fades away, Mateo? You're a guy with a strong libido. Will you start casting your net a little further afield? Because that would be something I would find intolerable.'

'You have my word. I am more than prepared to fold away that net and never bring it out of storage.

I would be one hundred percent faithful to you.' He paused and then said in a driven undertone, 'And that's presuming I tire of you. You might find that you're the one who tires of me…or we both might discover that the magic we shared in Italy is longer lasting than expected.'

Maude felt the persuasive impact of his words swirling round her, enticing her to agree with his proposition. Wasn't he right? Wasn't their child the only one that mattered?

But then she thought of her own parents and the love they shared, the intimate jokes between them, the way they still held hands.

Those were the simple things that came with love, things that could never be replicated in a relationship which would only ever be an arrangement, whatever words he used to describe it. *That* was what a child deserved, not a business arrangement between two polite parents, where resentment would most probably find its home in due course, whatever Mateo might believe to the contrary.

'So,' he urged. 'Will you marry me, Maude?'

She looked at him steadily, and then said as gently as she could, 'I can't, Mateo. I can't marry you.'

CHAPTER EIGHT

FIVE DAYS LATER Mateo swept by in his sports car to collect Maude from her house.

During that time, all talk about marriage had been dropped. He'd proposed once, tried to persuade her once, had been knocked back once and had retreated.

Was Maude happy?

Of course she was! Why wouldn't she be? Wasn't this exactly what she wanted? There was no way she wanted to be pressured into a situation that would never make sense in the long run!

Yet, she couldn't stifle a sting of disappointment at his hasty retreat. Obviously, whatever he'd said, once his obligatory offer had been rejected, his conscience had been cleared and he'd probably breathed a sigh of relief. He'd done the honourable thing and it wasn't his fault that she had turned him down.

He phoned her daily. How had her day been? Was there anything she needed?

Maude knew that there was a continuing conversation to be had, but she was putting it off, because she had been knocked for six by seeing him again and had wanted to take a little time out to handle events that seemed to be rushing past her at speed.

They had agreed that they would see her parents together.

'I won't marry you,' she had said five days earlier. 'But, yes, it would be good for you to come with me when I break the news to my parents. We can explain that we've decided that we're better as friends but will remain committed to our child...'

Mateo had looked away, expression unreadable, and nodded. They would visit just as soon as her parents were back from the three-week holiday they had taken post-Nick's and Amy's wedding.

'Your father is very naughty,' her mum had told her with a breathless, girly giggle two days after the wedding. 'He just went ahead and booked it... said I needed to relax after all the stress of arranging the wedding. It's a Caribbean holiday, and he says it's about time he got to see his wife in a bikini on a beach with someone else doing all the running around. You know your father, a hopeless romantic.'

In the meantime, Maude figured, there would be ample opportunity for Mateo and her to handle all the practical arrangements, which had yet to be discussed.

Ample time for her really to gather herself and face the future without qualm or trepidation and to count her blessings—which were many, not least having supportive family around her and, yes,

Mateo, who had made it patently clear that he was going to take an active part in his child's life.

She had cruised along, coming to terms with a life turned upside down and accepting that Mateo would now be a permanent feature in it, if from a distance, and one that she would just have to get used to. His casual daily chats had put her at ease and given her hope that her wild heart might be tamed by the time they came face to face again. Which, she'd quietly hoped, perhaps might not be until just before her parents were due to return. After all, it made sense that, if *she* had to retreat to consider an altered future, then surely so did he?

Fat chance.

The evening before, he had phoned and announced that he would be passing by to collect her the following day.

'Around four,' he had said. 'And don't ask. It's a surprise.'

'I've had quite enough surprises to last a lifetime, Mateo,' she had told him. His burst of laughter down the end of the line had reminded her of all those times in Italy when that laughter had thrilled her to the bone, making her breath catch in her throat.

So now, watching the busy streets below from the window of her rented flat, she noted the black Ferrari and her heart skipped a beat.

She watched, savouring those illicit, forbidden few seconds as he swung his lean body out of the low, sleek car and headed for the downstairs front door.

He was dressed in black. Black jeans and a black, long-sleeved tee-shirt that managed to delineate every muscle.

Maude heard the buzz of her intercom and his disembodied voice announcing his arrival, and she took one quick glance at her reflection before taking her time to collect her backpack and run her fingers through her hair.

She wore jeans and a colourful stripy jumper and trainers. There was no sign of any bump and only a couple of days before she'd wondered what he would think as the pregnancy advanced and she turned into a barrage balloon.

It was one flight down to the front door. She paused and took a deep breath before opening it, and then had to remind herself how to talk in a normal voice as her eyes met Mateo's, pinning her to the spot and depriving her of speech for a couple of seconds.

How could one human being be just so beautiful? A light, cool wind had tousled his hair and he hadn't shaved. The shadow of dark stubble made him look even more heart-stoppingly dangerous.

'Ready?' he drawled, which brought her right back down to planet Earth.

'Where are we going?'

'Haven't I already told you that it's a surprise?'

He walked round, opened the passenger door to his car, waited as she lowered herself inside and then relaxed back in the leather seat.

'I figured,' he said huskily, swinging into the

driver's seat and starting the engine, which roared into life, 'That if Mohammed wasn't going to come to the mountain, then the mountain would have to come to Mohammed.'

'What do you mean?'

Maude shifted to look at him to find him gazing at her, one hand resting loosely on the steering wheel and an amused half-smile on his face.

'I mean,' he said softly, 'We haven't had a proper conversation about what happens next, and I was beginning to get the feeling that if I didn't do something about that then I'd be hanging around for ever, phoning you every day and waiting for you to open up the dialogue.'

Maude reddened.

'That's not true,' she protested. 'I just thought that you might need to have some breathing space to digest what's happened.'

'And that's very thoughtful of you but now, for me, sufficient digestion has taken place.'

She felt frustration, bewilderment and restless dissatisfaction butting up against the brick wall of her stubborn refusal to see where he was coming from.

She was no pushover, and Mateo had known to back off, to retreat back into an easy familiarity, because war was not the answer and was not going to get either of them anywhere. He could never give her that one big thing she insisted on.

He eased the car away from the kerb and along the narrow street. It soon became clear that, wherever he was taking her, it was out and away from London because she recognised the artery that led out to the M25 and M4.

Curious, Maude settled back as the fast car picked up speed, clearing the London traffic and heading out. It was a familiar route but, instead of taking the junction to get to her parents' house, he instead began navigating a series of side roads, passing through a couple of small villages which she didn't recognise.

When she glanced across at him, her heart fluttered.

'You're eaten up with curiosity, aren't you?' He half-smiled, glancing at her, but not for long, because the roads were now small and windy.

'I hope I'm dressed for whatever restaurant we're going to.'

'What makes you think I'm taking you out for a meal?'

'Where else?' Maude sighed. 'And you're right. We need to have a conversation about, well, the details…and I'm guessing you wanted somewhere quiet where you can hear yourself think.'

'London *is* an extremely noisy place, now that you mention it,' Mateo murmured. 'Noisy…cluttered…polluted. Actually, I'm not taking you to a restaurant—although, of course, we *will* need to eat at some point. I suggest we wait and see where we land.'

'Where are we going, in that case?'

'Ten minutes and all will be revealed.'

There was something thrilling about this mysterious trip. The car passed through a bank of lush, green trees with fields in the background and through yet another quaint town, big enough for a pretty square with a pond in the middle, white houses jostling in a ring around it with a church dominating the parade.

'I've never been here before,' Maude observed, drinking in the detail and loving what she saw.

'No? I thought you might have explored this part of the world. You know, family days out?'

'It's lovely.'

'Glad you like it.' He swerved away from the town centre, but only for a few minutes, before taking another left and there, in front of them, was a cottage.

It was pink with beams and an upper storey that curved in an arch and glinted with leaded, stained-glass windows. On all sides there were fruit trees and it was protected by a low brick wall, behind which a tangle of hedge seemed to be staging a takeover.

'What on earth is this, Mateo?'

Eyes glued to the picturesque property, Maude let herself out of the car and stood for a few seconds, taking in the sight.

'A recent acquisition, although not finalised, but it's fair to say I see no obstacles.'

'A recent acquisition?'

'Come tell me what you think.'

He had a key and he opened the door to a spacious hall, with a flag-stone entrance, myriad rooms spreading in various directions and a short staircase that led up to the top.

The smell was musty, the smell of a house that hadn't been inhabited for a while. There were signs of disrepair. Maude could spot each and every one from a mile off because she had a keen eye for those details.

But the musty smell, the flaky paint and the saggy floorboards were all minor technicalities that faded away, because everything else was just so charming.

The dimensions were perfect and she forgot all about Mateo as she embarked on a journey of discovery, looking into all the rooms.

They were cosy rooms with high ceilings, bay windows where a person could sit and gaze out at the tangle of greenery behind, with the creak of ancient floorboards in need of restoration…

There were six bedrooms, three of which were on the ground floor and looped in a horseshoe shape, circling a small, private courtyard with its own gurgling fountain and rose bushes running amok. The other three bedrooms were up the flight of stairs and overlooked the fields at the back. Each room had its own veranda.

Maude's imagination went wild. There was so much to do.

'This is nuts,' she said, tour finished, as he pushed open the door from the kitchen that led out to the patchwork-quilt garden at the back.

'What is?'

'This!' She waved her arms around helplessly and sneaked a look outside at the overgrown orchard and the open space.

'Sorry?'

'You can't just go and buy a house you know I'd like to win me over.'

'Ah…so what you're saying is that you like the place…'

'You know I do! It's…it's wonderful. Lots of work to do. Definite signs of damp here and there that need taking care of, and that staircase has seen better days.'

'Want to have a look around outside?'

'Mateo, it's not going to work!' She folded her arms and made herself look at him with firm resolution. 'If this is about trying to get me to marry you by seducing me with the perfect cottage, then it just can't work.'

'Because of the love angle…' His heart constricted. He was so used to winning yet so powerless to win this one important thing. He banked down the sour taste of impotence.

'Don't.'

'Well.' He leant into her and there was a smile in his voice. 'As it happens, this cottage isn't for you, my darling.'

'It's not?'

'It's for me.'

* * *

He took his time showing her round the parts of the cottage she had yet to explore, and the grounds, which were considerably more extensive than they'd appeared.

He had thrown her. He could feel her all at sea and on edge after what he had said.

Did she think that he would sit around passively, waiting for her to take the lead and tell him how she saw things panning out?

She had dropped a bombshell, and he marvelled that she had then seen fit to withdraw from the fray in the expectation that he would play along with that.

She was having his baby! It was a thought that filled his head every second of every minute of every day, and each thought fired him up with a protective longing he had never known existed in him.

Mateo didn't doubt her for a single second that he was the father. Why would he? For starters, he could uncomfortably remember those occasions when taking precautions had not seemed as urgent as it should have; when sheer, blind lust had overridden everything else, including caution.

She also wasn't the sort to fabricate anything because, as she had told him in no uncertain terms, she wanted nothing from him.

Except the one thing he could give no one.

But why couldn't she see everything else that he brought to the table? Not just financial security, but a willingness to put his life on hold for ever for the sake of their child?

How could he have failed to explain to her, to make her see just how important it was that personal preferences be put on the back burner when a baby became part of the equation?

Was he disingenuous in thinking like that? Yet, he couldn't help himself. There was nothing he could ever say in criticism of his father, who had stoically brought him up, sacrificing much along the way, and always doing his best to make up for the lack of a mother figure.

He had had a good upbringing in that respect, yet Mateo was now beginning to realise just how much mother's abandonment of her husband, her marriage and *of him* had affected him down the years.

He had shut the door on love. Had the very fact that he had been born driven his mother away? On every level, that made no sense, but still, buried deep in his subconscious, was that fear which had driven him into barricading himself behind a steel fortress, protecting himself from the vagaries of emotions and everything that went along with succumbing to them.

But, more than that, he had realised just as soon as she'd told him she was pregnant that there was some yearning he had grown up with which he had never recognised to somehow fill the void in his life. He would never have dreamt of courting the roller-coaster ride of fatherhood but, now it had been thrust onto him, he was overwhelmed by a feeling of wanting his child to have what he hadn't had—the stability of a home with two parents.

Yet, Mateo was honest enough to realise that there was justification to Maude's refusal to get on board with that notion. The scars he carried weren't hers and what she proposed was what anyone who wanted more from marriage than a simple, practical, workable union between two people for the sake of the child they shared would do.

They would both be there for their child, which was more than he had had. There would be no shortage of love.

Unfortunately, for Mateo, that wasn't enough because he could easily think beyond that to a scenario he didn't intend to accept. He thought about her finding Mr Right, if such a guy existed, leaving him to be the father who showed up every other weekend while some other man effectively got to bring his child up as his own.

That wasn't going to happen.

But neither could Mateo force her to accept his marriage proposal. These weren't Victorian times, and he certainly wasn't dealing with a wishy-washy damsel who was in search of rescue.

That said, this cottage was step one in persuading her that, whilst it might not be her first choice, what they had was good enough to stay the course. Better, indeed, than merely *good enough*.

He would be patient and let her come to her own conclusions and, in the end, if she dug her heels in, then he knew that he would have no option but to retreat, however much that retreat would feel like a journey walked on broken glass.

But he had no intention of retreating until he had given it all he'd got.

'So, you're saying that this cottage is for *you*…'

'That's exactly what I'm saying.'

'You're a city guy, Mateo. Do you honestly expect me to believe you would be comfortable living out here, in the middle of nowhere?'

'The M4 is a hop and a skip away,' he pointed out, the very voice of reason. 'And, as you well know, a lot can be achieved virtually. These aren't the bad old days when we were all nailed to desks.'

'Were you ever *nailed to a desk*?'

'Fortunately, that fate passed me by.'

'You never told me that you were planning on buying a place out here.'

She'd swung round to look at him, hands on her hips, the overhanging apple tree throwing her into a mosaic of shadows.

Around them the air was rich with the smell of fruit and the dampness of earth, leaves, trees and nature. It was a garden that had run wild.

'I didn't realise I had to, considering we'll be going our separate ways,' Mateo said with a show of puzzlement, and watched her flush in response. 'While you were doing your thinking over the past couple of days, I was likewise doing something thinking of my own.'

'Oh yes?'

'Is there anything else you want to see while we're here?'

'No. Thank you.'

'In that case—' Mateo glanced at his watch '—we can go and have an early dinner somewhere local before we return to London.' He held up his hand even though she hadn't said anything in return. 'And no point telling me that you want to get back now. Whether the time suits you or not, we have to hammer a few things out, Maude, and I suggest we start doing that today—now that you've been shown around the first step I've taken in dealing with this situation.'

Mateo waited for her to object and, whilst he waited, his eyes drifted over her face and then he lowered them to her still flat stomach and felt the tug of something bigger and more powerful than he could ever have imagined possible.

He clenched his jaw, hooked a finger over his jeans and raked one hand through his hair.

'I suppose you're right.' She sighed and, without realising, cast one last wistful glance at the cottage, which was so damned perfect in every way imaginable.

'Right. There's a nice little place by the village green…'

'You've checked out the town?'

'When I do something, I make sure I do it properly.' He began leading the way back through the cottage and out to the front while she fell into step with him. 'No point liking a property only to discover once you've moved in that the neighbours are too loud and half the town's boarded up.'

It was a short drive to the centre. Along the way, he made sure to point out various plus points, just in case they'd passed her by. There were many ways to get what he wanted, and persuasion could be a powerful tool.

It would be an easy stroll to the centre of the town, even though they'd chosen to drive, Mateo told her. There were scenic parks within shouting distance and a vibrant community spirit, judging from the central square, the array of independent shops and businesses that made such a change from the monotony of chain stores and coffee shops.

He could have gone on, but he felt as if he was beginning to sound like an estate agent with an eye to a sale, so he fell silent as they strolled to the restaurant he'd sourced, letting her make up her own mind about the place.

It was hard not to enjoy the surroundings. They were the very essence of the picture-perfect English market town. They strolled past a butcher, a fishmonger and two greengrocers, all shut at the moment, but all promising top-quality fare, judging from the pristine awnings and cheerful signage. The coffee shops were likewise closed, but a buzzing atmosphere remained because there were restaurants aplenty and at least three pubs that all seemed to be doing booming business.

The restaurant was nestled down one of the side streets and was already filling up by the time they were shown to seats towards the back and orders were taken for some light food.

The garden was coming alive, making the most of the last of the summer days, with a string of fairy lights hooked up between trees and lanterns on tables.

Mateo was quietly satisfied with the choices he had made.

'So…' Maude said, a little awkwardly. 'You said you were going to surprise me and you did.'

'In a pleasant way, I hope?'

'How did you manage to find that place in the space of a few days?'

'I got a team of people to do it for me,' he confessed. 'I told them the sort of thing I wanted, that money was no object, that I wasn't afraid of renovations from the ground up, that speed was of the essence and hey presto.'

'Hey presto indeed…'

'The way I see it,' he mused slowly, sitting back while the waitress poured some water and a glass of wine for him, 'Is, whilst you haven't yet made clear whether you intend to continue living in London, I certainly think that some open space is a must. London is fine for the urban professional but in a few months' time I will no longer be just that urban professional. I'll be a father and with that comes certain conditions that I am more than happy to fulfil.'

'Right. Well, I hadn't got round to thinking…'

'About where you were going to bring up our child?'

'It's still some time away,' Maude said vaguely.

'So it is,' Mateo drawled in response. 'However, as you can see for yourself, the cottage is in desperate need of work. I suspect the purchase will be finalised within weeks and I already have a team on standby to descend the minute the signatures are in place.'

'That's very efficient,' Maude said faintly.

'I like to think so.'

'And you're going to move in…immediately?'

Mateo shrugged. 'I can't see why not. Naturally, I will maintain my place in central London, but the truth is I can always go there on the days when I won't be able to see my baby.'

'You make it sound as though I'm planning on keeping our child from you, and I'm not,' Maude said irritably.

'My mistake.' He gestured, an elaborate, rueful shrug, and smiled as she narrowed her eyes and viewed him with suspicion. 'Apologies if that's how it sounds. At any rate, yes, to answer your question. I'll be here whenever it's my turn. I'll have a nanny on call, and naturally I'll make sure you approve of my choice, although I intend to tailor my working to maximise the time I can spend with my child.'

He lowered his eyes and paused fractionally, and

when he returned to the conversation his voice was serious and thoughtful. 'I have a couple of ideas for development in the area, as it happens. Could work. There are some natural underground springs here that could be put to use, and of course it will certainly be a way of integrating within the community. As a single father on his own, it'll be important to get some sort of social life going.'

'I beg your pardon?'

'Well,' Mateo pointed out reasonably, 'We're both in changed circumstances, and for the first time in my life I do concur that my free and easy bachelor days are at an end.'

Their eyes tangled.

Maude felt a frisson of *something*. She knew that she was being asked to join dots but she had a cold feeling that she wasn't going to like the big picture.

'Yes, well, that was never my intention.'

'What was never your intention?'

'Like I told you when I…er…came to see you to tell you about the baby, I wasn't asking anything of you. I had no intention of disrupting your life.'

Mateo's eyebrows shot up.

'That was a little short-sighted, Maude.'

'There's really no need for you to…to…'

'Ah, but you're missing the point, my darling.' His eyes hardened. 'There is *every* need to. You obviously thought that you were dealing with a different kind of guy when you broke the news to me. You maybe thought that you were dealing with someone with very elastic moral guidelines.'

'Of course not!'

'You're not. I may have enjoyed myself playing the field, because I never had any interest in settling down, but that never meant that I was someone who might be happy to relinquish responsibility in a situation like this in favour of continuing with my old patterns of behaviour.'

His dark eyes glittered like jet and absolute intent was stamped on every feature. 'Like I said, I grew up in a single parent family. I know what it's like to long for what I saw other kids have—two parents. It's one thing for two people to end up divorced, for whatever reason. It's a completely different matter for a child to have never been given a window into what a united family might look like.

'You've made your mind up, and I can't frog march you up an aisle, but I *can* and *intend to* do everything within my power to make this situation as good as possible for the child we will share. It therefore goes without saying that my days of playing the field are over. In due course, I will doubtless find someone with whom to build a unit. It might not be the ideal unit, but it will be a unit. As you say, it's a sign of the times—children moving between families, bonding with step-brothers and-sisters. These things happen. Life goes on.'

Maude's mouth dropped open as these bare facts were laid out before her with ruthless efficiency.

What had she expected?

Had she thought that he would somehow remain in a vacuum, a part-time father doing his own thing, accommodating her while she got on with her life and conveniently never settling down?

Here he was. He had willingly taken the first of the big steps and he wasn't sorry about it, wasn't voicing any regrets for the lifestyle he'd be leaving behind.

He would move into the perfect cottage, having thrown money at it, with the perfect garden where a perfect kids' swing set would sit nestled amidst perfectly pruned apple and pear trees, and he would integrate into the community, doubtless becoming the man of the moment and the resident of the year.

Why wouldn't he? He was beyond wealthy, interested in doing his bit for the town and eligible beyond description.

Maude felt faint at the picture gathering shape in her head. Women would be falling at his feet. A sinfully rich, sinfully handsome guy without a wedding ring on his finger, pushing a baby in a pram and in search of a partner? The queue of women lining up to net him would stretch for miles. All that would be needed to finish off the enticing image would be a cute puppy on a lead in tow.

Her heart was thundering inside her.

He thought that *she* would likewise move on in her search for Mr Right because wasn't that the whole point of her rejecting his marriage proposal—the fact that she wanted love to be part and parcel of the deal?

He would never be constrained by concerns like that. A man who wasn't in search of love could easily find a suitable wife, and she could see that he would be a faithful and principled husband.

'You've gone a little green round the gills, Maude. Have something else to eat and we can change the subject, move on to less contentious issues. Although, in fairness, it is a subject we will have to return to at some point...'

Maude's anxious gaze collided with concerned dark eyes and she licked her lips, debating which way forward to go.

What had she done? Could she really spend a lifetime watching as Mateo, this guy she loved with all her heart, settled into a life from which she would be excluded? Life with another woman by his side— how on earth would she ever be able to bear that?

In pursuit of the ideal, what would she end up sacrificing and what would their child end up missing out on?

She had seen the situation through hopelessly blinkered lenses. Presented with a marriage proposal she had never envisioned—a proposal where no words of love had been exchanged, no passionate getting down on one knee and asking for her hand— she had fast forwarded to a vision of a miserable marriage in which her heart ached permanently for what she wanted and what was on offer. Mateo, growing restless, would descend into resentment about a situation he hadn't asked for and, trapped in the middle, good intentions or no good intentions, a child would bind them together.

How happy would that childhood be? she had asked herself. Kids picked up on stuff. In time, when everything inevitably fell apart, how much more damage would they inadvertently have caused?

She had stuck to her guns because everyone deserved love and marriage, whatever the circumstances, should never be a trap. She had failed to see a middle ground, which was the one Mateo would now occupy. One in which there could be contentment, harmony and…who knew?…over time, maybe not the crazy love she had for him but something like love, couldn't there?

The alternative…the one he had just presented to her, made her blood run cold.

She felt very green round the gills indeed when she thought about that.

'No,' she said in a strangled voice. 'We have to talk.'

And, looking straight into her eyes, watching the shadows flit across her face, Mateo knew that he had succeeded. He'd never contemplated marriage before but it was coming at him now.

He was ready to embrace it.

'Marry me, Maude,' he urged huskily. 'Step up to the plate and do what you surely must know is the right thing to do. Trust me.' He covered her hand with his. 'You will not want for a better husband, nor our child a more devoted father…'

CHAPTER NINE

SHE'D THOUGHT THE proposal had been a one-off but now Mateo's eyes glittered with intensity.

Had the same thoughts crossed his head? Even as he had told her that he would one day find a woman to complete the circle, had he thought about how he would feel if *she* likewise found a man to complete her circle?

He had proved that he would do whatever it took for the baby she was carrying. The sacrifices he had laid bare for her were enormous. With that would surely come a sense of fierce possession? Had he recognised that it would be difficult to absorb the thought of another guy in his child's life?

Had there been an element of cunning blackmail in that vivid prediction he had given her of life with baby? Had he banked on the brutal truth weakening her defences, making her see just what the repercussions would be if she walked away from the offer on the table?

There were a lot of other things he could have said

and was probably thinking. What would happen in the future if their child were to find out that marriage had been on the table but had been rejected out of hand? Would judgements be made?

Maude knew that it was crazy to worry about something that might or might not happen in the years to come but one thing she certainly knew— her parents would never understand. No one would. She would be on her own in that respect.

She would never find anyone else. She would be doomed to spend her days watching from the sidelines as Mateo got on with his life and replaced her with someone else. He would have no qualms about doing that. Why would he? He'd be a free agent in the emotional stakes when he couldn't love.

A wave of despair washed over her and, when it ebbed, she took a deep breath and met his dark eyes steadily.

'Why are you doing this?'

'Doing what?' He tilted his head to one side and frowned.

'Confusing me.'

'Because nothing in life is straightforward, Maude. We could pretend that we will remain the best of friends, amicably sharing custody, and then, when we find other partners doing all sorts of joint things together in a thoroughly modern way, but that won't be happening. Not on my part.'

'Is that some kind of threat?'

'No.' His voice was gentle but firm. 'Far from it. I would never stoop so low. I'm just being honest. I would find it very hard to watch another man make decisions about my child.'

Strip away the sentiment she was adamant about wanting, and the facts were laid bare. Why would he tiptoe around them? This was who he was—honest, forthright, and if he was a rock, immune to all that soft, woolly nonsense that ended up blowing away like gossamer at the first hint of an unfavourable breeze, then so be it. He could no more help being the man he was than she could help being the woman *she* was. Yet, with this baby in her, their worlds had to touch. He had shown her a vision of what would be if they didn't.

'I suppose,' Maude grudgingly conceded, 'I might find it difficult to watch another woman do things with my baby, my child.'

He held her gaze then lowered his eyes slowly and, when he next spoke, his voice was uneven.

'I'm really excited to see your body swell and grow with my child,' he murmured huskily and wild colour flared in her cheeks.

'If we decide to marry because of the situation, we shouldn't muddy the waters...'

'Those waters were muddied a long time ago. I think it's pointless trying to change that, don't you? Clear, open water has long disappeared and, I confess, I like it that way.' He smiled a slow, crooked smile that made her go weak at the knees.

* * *

Mateo was bursting with a deep-rooted sense of satisfaction. He could see a ring on her finger, his baby in her belly, unforeseen events that he didn't mind at all—not a bit. It would have been shocking if his brain wasn't currently wrapped up somewhere else.

'Let's go,' he murmured.

'Mateo…'

In response, Mateo reached to brush his finger across her cheek and watched as she shivered and blushed like a teenager. God, he'd missed that. Missed the way she responded to him.

'I've really missed you.' He breathed unevenly. 'Have you missed me?'

Caught between wanting to be cool and longing to be truthful, Maude gave a jerky nod.

She was going to marry this man and, like it or not, her heart was bursting with love and desire.

They didn't make it back to London. They made it out of the town, Mateo driving steadily with Maude's hand on his thigh, stroking in a way that made him clench his teeth as his erection pulsed steadily against the zipper. The first two villages they came to had offered nothing in terms of accommodation but the third had a pub with a sign advertising rooms and they made it in fast.

Small pub, small room, small bed…neither cared.

Mateo was stripping off the second the bedroom door was shut behind him. Maude's hands scrabbled over him, touching him everywhere, his chest, his shoulders, tracing the path down to where his erection was thick and rock-hard.

He couldn't get her clothes off fast enough and, as he stripped her of them, he whispered to her, voice thick with desire, stuff that made her skin burn and sent every pore in her body into instant, sizzling meltdown.

They stumbled their way to the bed and it creaked underneath them.

Her clothes were half-on, half-off, a barrier to his hands, which she wanted all over her.

'No need for protection,' he murmured as they fell on the bed, both naked, both hot for one another. 'It's liberating.'

'Yet we're here!' Maude laughed breathlessly. 'I'm having a baby, so it's safe to say we've been liberated before.'

'Touché.'

His hot gaze brushed her. He knelt and could only stare at her, lying naked for his hungry perusal. He rested his hand on her stomach.

'Have you…changed?' he asked.

'Changed how?'

'Your body. Does it feel different?'

Maude half-closed her eyes and thought that this might not be the real deal in terms of all her youthful dreams being realised—this might not be the fairytale ending she had always secretly longed for—but right now, with his dark eyes resting on her with interest and concern, things felt good.

He cared. Maybe not for her, but one hundred percent for the baby, and half a loaf was better than none at all.

'A bit. My...' she blushed '...my breasts are more sensitive,' she admitted. 'And I've gone off certain things. Coffee makes me feel a little sick...'

'Sensitive breasts,' Mateo murmured. He rounded them with his hands. 'They feel bigger.'

Maude laughed and went hot all over at the rampant hunger in his eyes as they rested on her.

'And they'll only get bigger.' She sighed. 'I'll look like a zeppelin.'

Mateo burst out laughing. 'Can't wait.'

Their love-making was slow, tender and thorough, making up for lost time, invigorated by a dimension to their relationship that hadn't been there before.

He touched her slowly, as though they had all the time in the world. He made her feel special. She wondered whether, subconsciously, he wanted to prove to her that what he had said was true—that they could have a good life together even though he didn't love her the way she wanted him to.

Afterwards, they lay curled into one another until he reminded her that there was still a little drive to London to do.

'Or we could just stay here,' he murmured. 'Now that you've reminded me of how much I've been missing, I might not be able to make it back to London without another stop somewhere.'

'I think we can manage it,' Maude murmured.

They did. Back to his place, which was another testament to his rise up the ladder, a marvel of blond wood, abstract art and pale furnishings.

It had been insightful of him to purchase the cottage, Maude thought as she walked around, running her hands along the white leather sofa and plunging her bare feet into the springy pale rugs. A toddler would wreak havoc in a place like this.

'That talk you mentioned we need to have…' She wandered towards him, looped her hands around his neck and drew him towards her.

'I can't say I'm in the mood for talking.' He kissed the tip of her nose and she smiled.

'Okay. Me neither. But Mum and Dad are back week after next. As soon as they're back, we can go and break the news.'

And with that Maude knew that there was no going back. She cupped the nape of his neck and leaned up to kiss him, then she kissed him a little bit more until she found she just couldn't stop.

It was drizzling two weeks later when they pulled into the courtyard outside her parents' house.

During that time they had talked and had the necessary conversations, sorted out where they would live and how that would work.

And they had made love.

On the surface, things couldn't have been better. Mateo had wanted his ring on her finger. He would get what he'd wanted. He'd shown her the down side of a relationship spent sharing custody, working out where weekends were spent and then, eventually, the messy business of other people having a say in the upbringing of the child he and Maude shared.

When he had put a bid on that cottage, then when he had taken her there, he had known just how much she would fall in love with it.

At heart she was a romantic, in love with the notion of being in love, and that cottage had all the hallmarks of just the sort of dreamy, fairy-tale place that would appeal to someone with a romantic heart. The urgent renovation element had added to the attraction.

When he'd told her that the cottage was meant for him, as his permanent residence once the baby was born, he had known that she would be swayed. Her imagination had gone into overdrive and it had accelerated even more when he had described the idyllic life of rural perfection he was effortlessly going to achieve, a life in which a suitable wifely candidate would barrel along within weeks, eager to take up the mantle of mother-figure.

Mateo had almost bought into the fantasy himself. In fairness, he would have made it work if Maude had stuck to her guns, but he had been over the moon when she had buckled and accepted his marriage proposal. He was a cool guy with a cool head and he had got what he'd wanted the cool way.

So why was this thread of unease running through him now?

* * *

'Are you nervous?' he asked, killing the engine and turning to look at her.

'Nervous?' Maude frowned but then smiled, doing her best to wipe out the vague sadness that had lodged inside her ever since she had accepted his marriage proposal.

She hadn't made a mistake. What she was doing was the right thing to do for a thousand reasons, not least because it was unbearable to think of this guy who had stolen her heart settling down with another woman.

Their child would have the sort of stable upbringing every child deserved, and she was in no doubt that Mateo would make an excellent father. Because it had become patently clear that he really cared about the baby. He might never have envisaged settling down with *her* or even prolonging what they had, however much he told her how much he still desired her and how much he had missed her, but he was fully engaged in his duty and she was the essential add-on.

She was and always would be the responsibility he had taken on board because he'd had no choice, not when he wanted the whole package with the whole full-time, hands-on two parents in the family unit he had never got the chance to have himself.

She had bowed her head and said goodbye to the dreams she had had growing up, and the reality of the life she was embarking on had settled like a mantle over her, spreading a sadness that she knew would never really go away, however much she told herself that she had done the right thing, the *only thing*.

Her body might still come alive when he touched it but it came alive because she was in love with him, because it wasn't just about desire.

'About breaking the news to your parents.'

'No.' She smiled with more genuine warmth. 'They're going to be over the moon, and when Nick and Amy find out they will be as well, although they might be a bit miffed that we beat them to it.'

'Then why have you been so quiet on the trip here?'

'Have I?'

'Are you having…second thoughts?'

'No,' Maude said firmly. She cupped his face with her hand and smiled, because this was the way ahead and she was going to make the very best of it. She was going to enjoy what she had been given and not allow herself to be plagued with regret for what she would never have.

'Sure?'

'Of course I am.' She hesitated. 'What, out of interest, would you do if I told you that I *was* having second thoughts?'

'I would try and dissuade you. There's no way I would throw the towel in without a fight.'

'And all that because of the baby?'

'That's right. Why else?'

'Why else indeed?' Maude murmured, fighting

back the sting of tears, knowing that time would take the sharp edges off and put everything into perspective.

'And don't tell me that there aren't distinct upsides to this situation…' He reached for her wrist and held her hand gently, turning it so that it was palm up and he could kiss the sensitive skin there.

On cue, Maude's whole body went up in flames. She sighed and her eyes darkened. Mateo looked at her with wolfish intent. 'I see you get where I'm coming from. Shall I spin the car around and we can find ourselves a nice little B&B ten minutes away? I'm sure your parents wouldn't mind if we're running an hour or two late.'

'You're terrible and, yes, they would send out a search party. I was so keen to fix a date to see them as soon as they came back that I'm sure they suspect something's up, and knowing my mother, she'll be bristling with all sorts of theories.'

Mateo relaxed because this was more certain ground. He didn't like it when he sensed something in Maude, something deep inside unvoiced. He couldn't deal with the nebulous suspicion that somewhere inside she was hurting. He hated the thought of that. This was much better.

'Well, if you insist.' He vaulted out of the car, loose-limbed, sexy and compelling and swung round to open the passenger door for her. When he helped her out, it was another reminder of the role she now played in his life—mother of his unborn child.

Her parents were waiting. The front door was flung open before Maude had time to reach for the door bell. Her finger was raised and poised to press it when her mother was standing in front of her, as brown as a berry, her hair even more white-blonde than ever and reshaped into a perky, shorter hairstyle.

'Maude!'

Her father was beaming in the background, ushering them in and making a fuss.

They looked like what they were, two people just back from a holiday in the sun.

'Mum, you *do* know that there's such a thing as sun block?' Maude teased, laughing and hugging them and then standing to one side while Mateo did the usual and blended in as though he had known them his entire life.

He was so at ease and so drop-dead gorgeous in a pair of black jeans and a cotton tan and black jumper and loafers. He was effortlessly sophisticated. He had told her about his childhood one night when they had been lying in bed, wrapped around one another while the last embers from their passionate love making had died down.

'I grew up with nothing materially,' he had said pensively, stroking her hair as she rested on his shoulder, curled into him like a cat. 'And where I came from there was a choice of two roads to travel down to sort that out—drug dealing or pulling yourself up by your bootstraps and doing the hard graft to get to the top.'

'Was it tough going against the grain?'

'Less so than you might think. My father was great when it came to the straight and narrow. He'd clocked the importance of money the minute my mother jumped ship for a rich guy. He might not have been able to achieve wealth himself but he made damned sure that I was on the right track to have a go at it myself, and I did.'

'I had it easy.' Maude had sighed with a pensive frown.

'Not that easy,' he had murmured, 'Or else you would have ended up married to a rich man a long time ago and your career would have been knowing how to fold napkins and lay a good table.'

'That's a stereotype!' But she'd burst out laughing and thought how good it was to be wrapped up in this man, so big, so dominant, so self-assured, a guy with a strong sense of duty and a deeply ingrained moral compass.

Whatever he'd grown up with or without, his father had been the bedrock when it had come to showing him the way forward, and he'd smiled when she'd told him, honestly, that she wished she could have met him.

That he was now the embodiment of everything that was uber-confident and crazily sophisticated showed just how much single-minded focus he had to get what he wanted out of life.

Such as power. Such as money. Such as this marriage, the passport to his child.

Maude felt his eyes thoughtfully watching her as they were ushered into the big family kitchen. Her mother was in her element, gesturing and describing their holiday while her dad smiled indulgently and went about the business of offering them drinks and nibbles, making the same well-worn jokes about having slaved to prepare the cheese sticks and dips, all of which were still in their wrapping.

'I would have done them myself,' Felicity said, 'But I didn't have the time. It's been a flurry of activity ever since we got back day before yesterday.'

They had migrated to the living room, which was comfortable and cosy with squashy sofas and a wide sideboard with framed family photos laid out along it, a parade of pictures depicting the sort of family life Maude had always envisaged for herself.

Her eyes slid away from the photos to clash with Mateo's. He was standing by the bay window, lounging against the ledge with a drink in his hand, legs lightly crossed at the ankles. Behind him, the back garden was shrouded in gloom, the days becoming shorter and announcing that autumn would soon be drawing in.

Their eyes held and, for a few moments, it felt as though time was standing still, allowing him to get inside her head and see the sadness that had lodged there.

Then they were both brought back down to earth by her mother clapping her hands, almost as though she was addressing a crowd of people, bringing them to order.

'I know you two have something to tell me!' She beamed and turned to her husband. 'Don't we, darling? And you must be absolutely fed-up hearing about the holiday...'

'Wait until the photos get developed,' Richard Thornton said. 'Brace yourselves for a repeat performance, but tack on another hour poring over the snapshots.'

'Mum.' Maude smiled, very much aware that Mateo had strolled towards her, joining her on the sofa, his thigh against hers, his legs spread as he relaxed back, 'I didn't think anyone actually developed photos in this day and age.'

'Darling, you know I like putting everything in frames!' She smiled and winked at Mateo. 'I'm not a fan of scrolling through a phone to look at pictures.'

Mateo was smiling good-naturedly, duly glancing at the array of family snapshots on the sideboard and knowing that, if he did a thorough house inspection, he would find many dozens more strewn on surfaces in all the rooms.

This was what he had missed out on. These were all the tangible, physical manifestations of the life he had never had, however good his father had been when it had come to raising him. And this was what Maude had wanted for herself, the big thing she felt she had sacrificed, the thing that only love could bring to the equation.

The moment passed by, leaving an uncomfortable taste in his mouth. Felicity, having got their undivided attention and having moved away from the holiday chit chat, fixed them both with a beady stare.

'Okay, don't tell me that you two love birds have hurried over here at full pelt because you couldn't wait a minute longer to hear about our holiday abroad. I know that can't be true because I usually have to force this young lady to come visit us...'

She grinned and rested her hand lightly on her husband's knee, an unthinking gesture of affection. 'I'd say spit it out right now, but Nick and Amy are popping over for supper, so if you have urgent news then maybe it can wait until they come? Which will be in...remind me what time they're coming, darling?'

'They'll be here in fifteen.'

'So, can it wait?'

'Mum, since when do you have to *force* me to visit?'

'Perhaps I exaggerated a little.' Felicity smiled and blew Maude a kiss.

'Well,' Maude began, 'As it happens, we *have* got...er...'

She was interrupted. The doorbell went and that was good. No, she was not going to back out of this agreement now, but the enormity of what she was embarking on was dawning on her. In thirty years' time, would she and Mateo have photos proudly displayed on every surface conceivable? Would they be taking romantic trips together? Or would their very functional relationship have evolved into two separate people leading separate lives, sleeping in separate quarters in the very big house only huge amounts of money could buy? Would they even still be together?

Maude knew this was a pointless direction for her thoughts to take but she was still tussling with them when Amy appeared in the doorway and Nick behind her, his arm around his wife's waist, her head leaning back on his shoulder, both smiling, both radiantly happy.

Mateo watched this family gathering at its most relaxed, very different from when he had last seen them all at that pre-wedding do, and held back as Maude stood to move towards her brother and sister-in-law, along with her parents.

He had got what he wanted.

He had never felt the drive to be possessive about anyone in his life before. He had become an island, strong, powerful and utterly shatter-proof. Cassie had been his one and only weakness and, even then, he had never given her anything more than his sympathy. But this baby... From the minute he had known of its existence, Mateo had realised that he would do his utmost for it, and that included marrying a woman who, to be brutally honest, had had no interest in marrying *him*. He had been given a deck of cards and he had known how to play them to his benefit.

But Maude had been out of sorts on the drive here. Had the prospect of seeing her parents again wakened her to what she was in the process of giving up?

He had watched her and, for the first time, he had realised that when it came to anything that involved emotion nothing was black and white. In *his* world, the world he had created for himself, there were no shades of grey. When he had decided that marriage was the solution to what had been thrown at him, that too had been a black and white decision.

But he had looked at those photos on the sideboard, had watched Maude as she had looked at them, and had felt as though he'd been given an insight into how she thought without her having to say a word. It had been a sucker punch to his gut.

And then when Nick and Amy had come in, the very picture of happiness, he had seen the shadow that had flitted over Maude's face. She'd smiled and moved, arms open to hug, but something inside her had crumpled and it had crumpled because of him.

He was the one who had given her a chilling alternative to the perfectly reasonable picture she had painted of two adults leading their own lives while still loving the child they had accidentally created together. He was the one who had swayed her into thinking that it was okay to give up on the dream of a happy family she'd probably had since she was a kid because of a baby.

But now Mateo had had an insight into just what that meant. It meant taking away her chance to find someone she loved, who loved her back. It meant taking away her chance to follow in her brother's footsteps and aim for the happy-ever-after life, whilst he had given up on all of that a long, long time ago.

In the flurry of activity, and with Nick and Amy demanding all the holiday info Maude and him had already been given, Mateo took the opportunity to pull Maude to one side as everyone else trooped into the kitchen where the drinks and nibbles had been left on the kitchen table.

'You're having second thoughts.'

'No,' Maude said honestly. 'I'm not.'

'I can see it on your face, Maude.'

'What can you see, Mateo?'

'Being back here…seeing your parents, seeing your brother and his wife… Has the reality of what lies ahead kicked in for you? Have you discovered that you don't like the image you're looking at?'

'That's not important.' Maude looked down. She could feel a dull throb in her temples as she stared at his expensive shoes, knowing that to follow that line up, to follow the line of his beautiful body, would be a little heart-breaking just at the moment. She quickly raised her eyes to his face and looked at him steadily.

'You were right. What's important is the life that both of us can work towards to make sure our child has the best possible start. If that means…' Her voice trailed off.

'If that means sacrificing our personal chance for real happiness and everlasting love with someone else, then so be it?'

Maude shrugged. Her eyes were welling up.

'This isn't the time for this conversation,' she said unhappily. 'I don't know why we're having it. I… I've already thought about this and made my mind up, come to terms with it, and I'm not unhappy.'

But neither was she happy. The only thing that could make her happy was the one thing he couldn't give her.

'Maybe I'm the one with the second thoughts,' Mateo said quietly and this time her eyes widened and she drew in a sharp breath.

She had not expected this.

Shock and misery tore into her in equal measure as she realised in a flash that she had misread everything.

She'd concluded that Mateo was the commitment-phobe who had no interest in ever settling down, whose heart was buried under layers of ice, but maybe that was before he'd realised the enormity of becoming a father.

Had that shown him that love was more important than he had ever imagined? Had he made the case for the business arrangement where everything slotted in nicely, papering over the fact that he didn't love her, presuming that she didn't love him either, only to gradually realise that, for a true family unit to stand a chance, feelings had to be part of it? That love had to be part of it?

Had *she* been the one to come to terms with the sacrifices he mentioned only for him to gradually come round to *her* point of view? The unfairness of that hit her like a punch in the stomach.

'What do you mean?' she questioned jaggedly.

'I think,' Mateo said in a low voice, 'That we need to spill the beans about our little charade that got out of hand. You were right, Maude. You…*we*…can very happily make a go of bringing up a child without, as you so graphically put it, being shackled together, sacrificing all chances of finding real, lasting, *loving* happiness with someone else.'

'I don't think I put it quite like that…' She drew in a shaky breath and tried for a smile, before continuing. 'You're saying that you've decided that you're ready to fall in love now?' She loosed a brittle laugh. 'I thought you were adamant that that sort of thing wasn't for you.'

Mateo shrugged. 'I guess you must be wondering about the things we discussed. The cottage…living there… Maude, the cottage is yours, unless you have any objections.'

Maude realised that she didn't want the cottage. She didn't want anything but Mateo. She had dug her heels in and turned him away when he had first proposed. He didn't love her, would never love her, and she had stuck her chin in the air and rejected what he had offered because it hadn't fitted in with the picture of the ideal dream life she had painted for herself.

Then she'd seen sense, but now he was the one turning away, and it showed her just how bleak and unforgiving the very future she'd originally demanded looked in the cold light of day.

She might have felt sad when she'd done her comparisons with what she was going to have and what her parents had, what Amy and Nick had, but the sadness she felt now was without compare.

Not that she could turn back.

'Let's go talk to your parents, Maude.' He smiled. 'It's what you wanted, isn't it? So now I'm going to make it real for you...'

CHAPTER TEN

FROM OUTSIDE, Maude could hear the buzz of voices and laughter.

Holiday anecdotes were being exchanged. Voices were talking over one another and there was lots of laughter, teasing and the thrum of a happy family life, the very family life she had longed for and was now saying goodbye to.

Next to her, Mateo's purposeful stride filled Maude with suffocating panic, but what on earth could she say? That she'd had a change of heart? That she loved him and would take him at any price?

In short, push him into a trap when he had now discovered that there might just be something more rewarding out there for him?

How proud she'd been! How determined to dig her heels in because things hadn't been perfect!

She pushed open the kitchen door to four faces that turned, beaming, in their direction.

'Mum.' She cleared her throat. Some of her unhappiness must have been mirrored on her face because the smiles dropped and she could see concern replace the laughter.

'What's the matter, darling?'

'We should have been honest with you from the beginning.' Mateo stepped in to take over, giving Maude a reassuring squeeze on her shoulder before swerving round to pull out a chair at the kitchen table, which he nodded to Maude to take so that he could stand behind her, his hands resting on the back of the chair while everyone stared at them in confused silence.

'Honest about what?'

Mateo gazed at the faces turned towards them. He had always been cool, collected, utterly in charge, but he could feel himself getting hot under the collar. He could feel Maude's tension flowing from her shoulders to his fingers like the buzz of an electric current.

This was for her.

He'd corralled her into following him but seeing her…watching what she saw and what she had always expected, all the things he had never really had a clue about…had done something to him. He had felt the twist of a knife in his gut and however determined he had been to get what he wanted, to drive the situation in the direction he felt it should take, that sick feeling he'd had watching her accept her dreams disappearing had changed everything.

'Honest about what?'

'Honest about the fact that, when I came here the

first time, I didn't come in the capacity of Maude's boyfriend, which you were led to assume.'

'What are you saying? What *is* he saying, Maude, darling? I simply don't understand.'

In an unwitting show of unity, her parents had edged closer together and were now standing side by side, arms touching, while Nick and Amy hovered on the periphery, as bewildered as Felicity and Richard.

Maude and Mateo both rushed in, their voices overlapping. Maude could detect the high edge of hysteria in her voice and she fell silent, listening as Mateo calmly took over the monologue.

His voice was low and soothing, making everything sound so rational.

From start to finish. The arrangement made way back when…an optimistic solution to two problems. The problem of Maude not wanting to show up without an escort but facing the prospect of that because her plus-one had bailed on her. And Mateo's problem with his ex which had become an ongoing saga, drifting into the dangerous territory of her becoming a stalker, leaving him the unpleasant option of having to take hostile steps to deter her.

'It seemed straightforward at the time,' Maude said to a silent, open-mouthed audience. When her mother apologised for making her feel that she was somehow *lacking* because she hadn't followed the expected path, Maude felt tears prick the back of her eyes.

'I never thought…' her mother said. 'I should have

been a little more thoughtful. Darling, I so hope you can forgive me. You know I've only ever wanted the best for you.'

Mateo's jaw tightened. The family love around him was a stark reminder of what he had not had, and he kept focused on that, focused on powering past the desperate urge to do whatever it took to hang onto Maude, to build the life he wanted to build.

Without the love. Because he was incapable of loving anyone. He was too tough, too cold. Those doors had been firmly shut a long time ago.

Hadn't they?

Something shifted inside him and for a few seconds he lost the power of speech.

He felt his hand tighten on her shoulder and had to make an effort to loosen his grip. But he just couldn't remove his hand because he wanted to carry on touching her.

Maude and her mother were smiling patchily, half-laughing and sighing, going over old ground, talking about misunderstandings, both knowing that those misunderstandings were trivial in the great scheme of things because there was sufficient love between them to more than make up for them.

Mateo heard Maude pick up the thread of the conversation, returning to the charade they had cooked up between them. He noted the way she said almost nothing about Cassie. There was no hint of criticism of his ex who had been responsible for escalating the situation.

'She's a bit fragile, I guess,' Maude said vaguely, when pressed for details of how a fake engagement had come about, conjured up from thin air, or so it seemed. 'And you know how it is…she decided to be a little naughty, I'd say.'

Smart, sassy, soft as marshmallow underneath, kind, generous…

Mateo felt the steady beat of his heart and his pulses quickened.

He wasn't interested in relationships. He was interested in fun, in sex. In ships that passed in the night. Those were things he had made absolutely clear to Maude from the start, as if they hadn't been clear already.

She knew his history. She knew that staying power wasn't in his remit. Besides, it was self-evident that he wasn't her type and never had been. She'd more or less told him as much herself.

What they had should have been straightforward, so how was it that he was standing here, his heart was thumping and he was perspiring and in the grip of the disconcerting feeling that he was suddenly standing at the top of a very perilous precipice, looking down into an abyss?

'Cassie was one of my more monumental mistakes,' he cut in, moving to sit next to Maude and keeping the chair close to hers, although she didn't look at him as he did so.

Tension radiated from her in waves and he badly wanted to reach out and hold her hand but he wasn't sure how she might react. A lot of water had flowed under the bridge and they were here now facing a situation neither had anticipated, spilling the beans to the very people he knew she had hoped would never find out about her deception.

'She sounds very vindictive. All of this... I guess things might have been worse...'

That from Amy, who then proceeded to marvel at the train of events that had led them to a phoney engagement and a world of coincidences while Nick watched her indulgently and affectionately.

'We never meant for things to go the way they did,' Mateo said quietly, capturing everyone's attention simply by the tenor of his voice. 'The engagement story broke and I decided that it might be an idea for Maude and I to disappear for a while. I have a house in Tuscany...'

'A mansion on an estate with vineyards attached,' Maude filled in wryly.

'Yes, one of those. Far from prying eyes, and handy, because I knew that there was some business there to take care of so I would be able to kill two birds with one stone. What happened was—'

'Wasn't meant to happen,' Maude jumped in hastily, avoiding eye contact with everyone and focusing instead on the kitchen clock on the wall.

'But it did, didn't it?' Mateo murmured, turning to look at her, satisfied when she reluctantly turned to look at him in return.

* * *

Just like that, the room shrank to just the two of them.

Maude had been aware of him moving from behind to sit next to her, with everyone else standing, so the focus of attention had been squarely on them. But she hadn't realised how close he was until now because she had been making such an effort to keep her eyes averted.

'And you said…' Mateo locked his eyes on hers '…that there were no regrets.'

'No,' Maude said with wrenching honesty.

'And…like a broken record… I maintained that what you saw was what you got with me.'

'You don't have to repeat the mantra, Mateo,' she replied jerkily, 'I got the message loud and clear.'

'How can I begin to tell you that it was a message I was so accustomed to churning out that it never occurred to me that the day might one day come when it was no longer on point?'

'What are you saying?'

She started when her father cleared his throat, and when she blinked back to reality it was to find her parents glancing at one another and shuffling.

'I do think,' her mother said briskly, 'That these two might want to have a conversation without us all around picking apart every word they're saying.'

Maude opened her mouth to vigorously deny any such thing but was overruled by Mateo, agreeing that he would appreciate a little bit of privacy.

At which point, all four sidled out, with her mother leading the way, and the kitchen door was shut quietly behind them. Maude turned to Mateo to ask what the heck was going on but he silenced her with a finger on her lips.

'Let me talk,' he murmured. 'This is hard for me to say but I need to say it.'

'No, you don't. We've said everything there is to say. We can tell them about the pregnancy, but the ground work…' Her voice trailed off. She couldn't finish the sentence.

'The ground work has only just begun, my darling.'

The way he said *my darling* sent a thrilling frisson through her which she loved and loathed at the same time.

'I told you that the message I always imparted was the same—no commitment. I wasn't interested. As it happens, you are the only woman to know why. At the time, I didn't even stop to question how it was that I had shared that confidence with you because it had seemed so natural.'

'And I understood, Mateo. I *understand*.'

'I don't understand,' Mateo admitted quietly. 'I don't understand how I could have allowed my past to dictate the future to the extent that I simply shut the door on any hope of having a meaningful relationship with a woman. I just never questioned it.'

'You were hurt as a child. How could you not be

affected? I don't blame you. I would have been the same, I'm sure.'

'You forgive too easily.' But he smiled crookedly at her and risked a light touch, his finger on her hand, letting it linger there for a few moments. 'I never anticipated going to bed with you, Maude, and, before you tell me the obvious, I know—you never anticipated going to bed with me either. Making love to you… It was mind blowing, like nothing I had ever experienced before. I told myself it was because you were so different from all the women I'd gone out with.'

'Tell me about it.'

'Appearances have nothing to do with it,' he admonished but gently, tenderly. 'I never got the appeal of a woman who enjoyed giving as good as she got, but of course you were always that woman. You never shied away from saying what you had to say when it came to work. You were always happy to shoot down anyone you thought had flimsy ideas on whatever structures you were working on and, if that person happened to be me, then that never stopped you from loading the gun.'

He paused and looked at her thoughtfully. 'Show me that woman and I would have told you that I wasn't interested because what I wanted was someone soothing and non-argumentative. Who needs extra stress when your work life is already stress-packed and lived in the fast lane? But how wrong I was.'

'Are you telling me that you enjoyed making love to me because of my mind?'

Oh, how Maude wanted to read a million and one things into every word leaving Mateo's beautiful mouth, but she had to keep a grip on reality. Was this all leading up to a convoluted explanation as to why he now wanted to give her the freedom she had demanded? Why he wanted to find his own way, begin his own search for a woman he could love?

'Or,' she whispered slowly, disengaging herself from the stranglehold of his dark gaze, 'Is this your way of kindly telling me that I set you on the straight and narrow.'

'Come again?'

'You're going to be a father, Mateo. You're entering a new chapter in your life. You might not have asked for it, but sometimes things happen not quite along the expected lines. Maybe that's opened your eyes to what I told you at the start. That a family unit is important, yes, but a family unit with all the right ingredients in place. Maybe going out with me for a while made you see that it's possible to have something with a woman who isn't afraid to argue with you…is that it?'

'Not at all.'

'What do you mean?'

'I mean that this is my way of humbly apologising for being a complete fool and bravely asking you whether you would consider marrying me for all those right reasons you talked about.'

'I don't understand what you're saying.' Maude looked at him in sudden confusion as the ground was swept away from under her feet, and the hope she had been keeping in check burst its banks and threatened to rampage over every iota of common sense she had done her best to put in place.

'I love you, Maude Thornton.'

'No, you don't. Don't say stuff like that, Mateo.' Her eyes welled up but she fiercely kept the tears in check. 'This isn't a game!'

'It's very much not a game, and if you'd look at me…' he tilted her chin so that she had no choice but to look at him '…you'd see that I'm being one hundred percent serious. Darling Maude, why do you think I suddenly decided that you were free to walk away?'

'Because…because…'

'Because I love you. We came here and I saw the way you were with your family, the way your family were with you. I realised that there was no such thing as black and white when it comes to family ties and the jumble of emotion that makes us stick at relationships, get married, have hope, believe in happy-ever-afters. I saw the sadness in your eyes and I knew that you were weighing up what you were sacrificing and what you were going to gain. Weren't you?'

It was a statement more than a question and Maude nodded imperceptibly. Her head was still buzzing with what he had just told her.

He loved her? How could that be? Dared she be-lieve him?

Yes. She did believe him. She could see the sin-cerity in his eyes but, that aside, she knew this man and knew that he would never, ever say anything like that as a ploy to getting what he wanted.

'I couldn't help it,' Maude admitted. 'But, how-ever sad I was at giving up on the dream of the per-fect life, I was still going to marry you because...'

'Because I made a great case for it?'

'Because, when I sat back and really thought about what life would look like without you in it, I...was scared.'

'Are you saying what I hope you are?'

'I'm saying that I fell in love with you and, by the time I realised, it was too late to start being ra-tional about it. It hit me like a sledgehammer.' She smiled ruefully but her heart was soaring and she was giddy with happiness. 'And then I found out that I was pregnant.'

'Maude, you've made me the happiest guy on earth. The minute you told me about the pregnancy, my whole world tilted on its axis, and suddenly ev-erything seemed to fall into place. I love you so much, my darling. So again, can I ask...will you marry me for all the right reasons?'

'Oh, Mateo!' Maude breathed, cupping his face with her hand. 'I think I can do that.'

'In which case, it's time we carried on this con-versation with your family...'

* * *

They married five weeks later. A wedding in Tuscany, where friends and family were flown over for the weekend, no expense spared. The wine was from home-grown grapes, the food had been lovingly prepared locally and Maude reconnected with some of the familiar faces she had seen when they had been there.

She could not have hoped for anything more wonderfully romantic. It was a small, intimate affair, just friends and family, not a reporter in sight. To think that they had escaped to this villa in Italy to avoid the glare of publicity instigated by a vengeful ex. Now the tabloid press was far too engaged dashing behind a minor royal who had been caught taking drugs and was facing a prison sentence to bother with their story. Indeed, their nuptials, duly reported without any gossipy fanfare, were announced in the discreet pages of the broadsheets and in the *Financial Times*.

She had seen the villa in the summer, but it was as spectacular in autumn, and Mateo had arranged for it to be wonderfully lit for the reception with fairy lights, lanterns and outside an elaborate, sprawling pergola entwined with flowers and slatted so that the moonlit, starry sky was visible when you looked up. The food was served there. It was perfect.

And then afterwards they'd moved into the cottage, which had been refurbished, and started on the business of preparing for the little arrival.

It was busy, joyous and dream-like.

* * *

Exactly six months after they were married, Maude woke to the dull throb of back pain. Lying in the king-sized bed, with Mateo curved into her, she watched this big man sleep and the love she felt for him was so huge that it brought a lump to her throat.

He would panic.

She smiled, but then winced, breathed in sharply and roused him, voice as calm as she could make it, to tell him that the time had come.

Mateo woke with the alacrity of a cat. He'd been waiting for this. He felt as though this was the very moment he had been waiting for his whole life and he flicked on the light switch, turned to her with concern and slid off the bed to get dressed, all without pausing to draw breath.

In his head, he had rehearsed everything a thousand times. He grinned when she said, casually, 'You're not going to panic, are you?'

Mateo looked at her, in the process of zipping his trousers, grinning.

'Do I strike you as the kind of guy who panics?'

'In a situation like this? Yep.'

At three-thirty in the morning, the roads were bleak and empty. It was a route Mateo knew well. Ever since they had moved to the cottage, he had become accustomed to roads that were largely free of traffic and had become accustomed to the way they spun and twisted round corners, often without

warning and with the occasional tractor meander-
ing along, not a care in the world for traffic piling
up behind it.

Once upon a time, he had been a workaholic and,
while he still worked hard, things had been put into
perspective.

Life had been put into perspective.

He reached out to briefly hold her hand and felt
her hang on tightly to it. He heard her trying to put
the breathing method she had been taught into practice. Panic? He was on the verge of it.

He had wanted to go private for the entire pregnancy, but Maude had burst out laughing and told
him not to be an idiot.

'We could have had a top consultant waiting for
us right now,' he ground out, swerving into the hospital car park and helping her out.

'This is just fine, Mateo. I can't begin to tell you
how many women successfully deliver their babies
without a top consultant on speed dial.'

Eight hours later, Violet Felicity Moreno was delivered without fuss.

And there in the hospital, as Mateo sat and gazed
in wonder at the tiny seven-pounds-and-eight-ounces
scrap of dark-haired baby girl lying next to his wife's
bed, he knew what peace, joy and contentment felt like.

It was something he thought he would never
achieve, something he had never even thought about,
a concept that had never cropped up on his horizons.

His beloved Maude was smiling at him, her love as unconditional for him as his was for her.

Happiness.

* * * * *

#4105 THE BABY BEHIND THEIR MARRIAGE MERGER
Cape Town Tycoons
by Joss Wood
After one wild weekend with tycoon Jude, VP Addison must confess a most unprofessional secret...she's pregnant! But Jude has a shocking confession of his own: to inherit his business, he *must* legitimize his heir—by making Addi his bride!

#4106 KIDNAPPED FOR THE ACOSTA HEIR
The Acostas!
by Susan Stephens
One unforgettable night with Alejandro leaves Sienna carrying a nine-month secret! But before she has the chance to confess, he discovers the truth and steals her away on his superyacht. Now, Sienna is about to realize how intent Alejandro is on claiming his child...

#4107 ITALIAN NIGHTS TO CLAIM THE VIRGIN
by Sharon Kendrick
Billionaire Alessio can think of nothing worse than attending another fraught family event alone. So, upon finding Nicola moonlighting as a waitress to make ends meet, they strike a bargain. He'll pay the innocent to accompany him to Italy...as his girlfriend!

#4108 WHAT HER SICILIAN HUSBAND DESIRES
by Caitlin Crews
Innocent Chloe married magnate Lao for protection after her father's death. They've lived separate lives since. So, when she's summoned to his breathtaking Sicilian castello, she expects him to demand a divorce. But her husband demands the opposite—an heir!

#4109 AWAKENED BY HER ULTRA-RICH ENEMY
by Marcella Bell

Convinced that Bjorn, like all wealthy men, is up to no good, photojournalist Lyla sets out to prove it. But when her investigation leads to an accidental injury, she's stranded under her enemy's exhilarating gaze...

#4110 DESERT KING'S FORBIDDEN TEMPTATION
The Long-Lost Cortéz Brothers
by Clare Connelly

To secure his throne, Sheikh Tariq is marrying a princess. It's all very simple until his intended bride's friend and advisor, Eloise, is sent to negotiate the union. And Tariq suddenly finds his unwavering devotion to duty tested...

#4111 CINDERELLA AND THE OUTBACK BILLIONAIRE
Billionaires of the Outback
by Kelly Hunter

When his helicopter crashes, a captivating stranger keeps Reid alive. Under the cover of darkness, a desperate intimacy is kindled. So, when Reid is rescued and his Cinderella savior disappears, he won't rest until he finds her!

#4112 RIVALS AT THE ROYAL ALTAR
by Julieanne Howells

When the off-limits chemistry that Prince Sebastien and Queen Agnesse have long ignored explodes...the consequences are legally binding! They have faced heartbreak apart. But if they can finally believe that love exists...it could help them face their biggest trial *together*.

Get 4 FREE REWARDS!

We'll send you 2 FREE Books plus <u>plus</u> 2 FREE Mystery Gifts.

FREE
Value Over
$20

Both the **Harlequin® Desire** and **Harlequin Presents®** series feature compelling novels filled with passion, sensuality and intriguing scandals.

HARLEQUIN
PLUS

Try the best multimedia subscription service for romance readers like you!

Read, Watch and Play.

Experience the easiest way to get the romance content you crave.

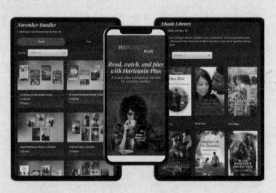

Start your **FREE TRIAL** at
<u>www.harlequinplus.com/freetrial</u>.